THE CASE FILES OF SAM FLANAGAN:

Opened Wounds

JUDITH WHITE

WCP

World Castle Publishing, LLC
Pensacola, Florida

Print ISBN: 9781629891903
eBook ISBN: 9781629891910
First Edition World Castle Publishing, LLC, January 1, 2015
http://www.worldcastlepublishing.com

Licensing Notes

Cover Artist: Scott Michael Foster
Editor: Maxine Bringenberg

Dedication

For Nora Reese White

Acknowledgments

I want to thank Tommy Burelle, owner of Tommy's Detroit Bar & Grill, for being such a gracious host to us. When visiting his establishment, he took us down to the basement to see first hand the tunnel leading to the church next door. During prohibition the Purple Gang transported their stock of illegal liquor into the church when alerted of an impending raid.

FOREWORD

Some years ago, my husband and I took a short tour offered by a local park service. The tour consisted of crossing the Detroit River in a small boat, stopping at the shores of Canada, and immediately returning. En route, our guide told fascinating stories of the prohibition era and those who controlled the liquor trafficking in the city of Detroit at that time. The infamous group was known as the Purple Gang led by the Bernstein brothers, and I had never heard of them.

The Purple Gang was a group, not unlike Al Capone and those in his organization, which terrorized the streets of the city of Detroit, Michigan in the 1920's and the early 1930's with their lawless endeavors. This story involves their activities, but for purposes of creativity, I've changed the names of the gang members. The names within this story are fictitious, as is the event described in "Opened Wounds: The Case Files of Sam Flanagan."

But who were they? The main members started out as school chums on the Lower East Side, getting themselves involved in petty thievery, pick-pocketing, and vandalism. As they grew older, their crimes became more serious. They soon graduated to armed robbery, gambling, loan sharking, kidnapping, extortion, murder, and bootlegging under the guide of older neighborhood gangsters.

Their main years of underworld control in Detroit were 1927 to 1932. It was a predominantly Jewish group and they were exceptionally violent. They were so ruthless that when Al Capone had visions of controlling Detroit, he nixed that idea in favor of a working relationship with the Purples to avoid a bloodbath. The mob raked in millions of dollars from their bootlegging alone. The men at the top were the Bernstein brothers, sons of Jewish immigrants. Abe Bernstein was the main leader, with his brothers Joe, Raymond, and Isadore (Izzy) close behind him in the ranks. There is one theory that they acquired their name from a conversation which took place between two Detroit shopkeepers, one business owner saying that the boys were not like other children of their age. They were tainted—off color. The other man agreed by responding that they were rotten, purple like the color of bad meat. They were a Purple Gang.

The gang's reign was short lived due to disagreement and arguing within its own ranks, warring with opposing gangs wanting to take control of the city, and finally, imprisonment for their crimes. Many Purple Gang members died inside the prison walls.

CHAPTER ONE

I wanted to have nothing to do with this case; nothing whatsoever! She'd waltzed into my office unaware of how even the mention of his name would affect me. She had opened wounds that had almost been healed when she told me her story. *Almost*. It was a story I never wanted to have mentioned to me again. Let me start at the beginning.

Flanagan Investigations–that's what the sign reads on my door. It's also stenciled on the window overlooking Woodward Avenue in the heart of downtown Detroit, Michigan. I've been renting this office for almost six years now. Prior to that, I was a cop for the city. I liked my job, but I didn't exactly follow directions or play by the rules. I'd committed nothing so egregious as to sink me into so much hot water that I couldn't crawl out, but my commanding officers had had it with me. I won't go into all the details, but I couldn't say I really blamed them.

After leaving the department, I took a couple of months off. I'd socked away enough money to be able to do that, which was damned difficult in those days. When I became bored out of my mind, there was enough money left over to open my own agency; just barely enough. So far, it had suited me perfectly. Oh, there were always those moments when I wished I'd gone into another field altogether, and there were periods when a case to work on was a rare thing. But it all evened out over time.

My name is Samuel J. Flanagan. Of course, the only one in my lifetime who ever called me 'Samuel' was my mother, and usually that was when she was angry with me. (Actually, that's not quite true—there was also Mr. Humphries, my sixth grade teacher. He called me "Samuel" all the time.) I'd been divorced for eleven years and had lived with my eighty-two year old grandmother, Ruby Flanagan, for the last ten of those. There had been a few times when I seriously thought about getting my own place, but for the most part, it had been a comfortable arrangement. Gran yelled into the telephone and made me read every piece of mail to her because of her poor eyesight, but other than that, she was as fit as a fiddle.

I'd just finished a case—if that's what you want to call it. For six days straight, I'd been dog sitting for a gentleman I'd made the acquaintance of back in the initial days of May. He called my office back then, pleading with me to go to Cleveland, Ohio to retrieve his dog—a Rottweiler named Daisy. He'd been through a nasty divorce, and when his ex-wife moved out, taking along all the judge had given her in the settlement, she also took what didn't belong to her—the man's four-legged best friend. Eight days ago he had once again called to hire me to stay at his house to watch Daisy while he flew to New York on a business trip. He would pay me my standard fee—ten dollars a day. Normally his maid would have performed this service, but she'd had a family emergency and would be away until mid-July. I had nothing better to do, so I jumped at it.

At our first meeting, Daisy and I had had an altercation. Driving back from Cleveland, Daisy on the front seat next to me, I sounded my horn at an ignorant driver who had cut me off in traffic. Little did I know that this would startle my passenger and she'd react by lunging at me and taking a chunk out of my right forearm. After competent medical attention, and a stop at a local butcher's, we were on our way again with an understanding. She'd sit in the back seat for the rest of the trip with a bone of her own to chew on.

During my six day stay at the home, the Rottweiler and I had gotten on much better; taking swims in her owner's pool several times a day, dining on steaks and seafood from his freezer, and sipping his premium scotch in the evening—well, we didn't share the scotch. I knew better than to serve a Rottweiler scotch!

Today I was wishing I was still staying at the place with the pool and the steaks and the scotch. For the past five days, the temperature had been in the ninety-five degree plus range. It was sweltering in my office as I tried to tidy up my files. I had the windows wide open, as was my door leading to the hall. It was all to no avail. No breeze moved through the atmosphere. I was about ready to call it a day when my phone rang.

"Flanagan Investigations," I said into the mouthpiece.

"May I please talk to Sam Flanagan?" came a loud voice that I recognized as that of my grandmother. I openly chuckled and passed myself the phone.

"Hi, Gran, this is Sam."

"Hi, dear, are you coming home soon?" she asked with excitement in her voice.

"Actually, I was just about to head out. Why, what's up?"

"Oh, nothing," she said, trying to act casual. "I just wondered when you'd be home." And then, as an afterthought, she added with slight panic in her voice, "You *are* coming straight home, aren't you?"

I laughed, "Yes, Gran. I'll be there shortly."

"Ask your friend to come along if you'd like," she said.

"Friend? What friend?" I furrowed my eyebrows, wondering what she was talking about.

"Your friend; the one who answered the phone, dear. Maybe he'd like to have supper with us, since we have nothing special planned for tonight."

I heard her try to muffle a snicker by putting her hand over the mouthpiece of the telephone.

I laughed again. "Okay, I'll see if he can make it."

And then we hung up. I had to smile. For the past two days, Gran had been trying to hide her excitement over the fact that she was planning something out of the ordinary for me. This morning she'd tried to act like it was a day just like any other, but she hadn't succeeded. She'd made comments such as, "Today is going to be a *good* day!" and "Ah well, I guess we can just relax tonight and do nothing." As if that was any different than many of our days. No, she hadn't fooled me. She had something in the works—she'd been planning something memorable; and when I arrived home, I'd find out what that something was.

Today, Friday, July 2, 1943 was my birthday. I'd been dreading the day for months now, but I'd awoken that morning feeling no different than I had the day before. There were no aches in my joints, no shortness of breath, no memory loss. I looked no different. I'd come to realize that turning forty wasn't so bad after all.

CHAPTER TWO

The windows were down all the way as I maneuvered the '38 burgundy Chevy through the busy streets of Detroit. The air that moved through the interior was oppressive and made it feel as though I was sitting in a sauna. I was sticky with a dampness that covered my whole body. Still, I couldn't help but anticipate what awaited me once I arrived home. I figured it this way—it was my fortieth birthday and that number was special. People were usually thrown parties for that particular birthday, and I figured that's what Gran had done. Who could she have invited? Bill "Mac" McPherson and his wife, Betty, for sure. He'd been my partner back at the precinct when I'd been on the force. She'd met Mac a number of times and just this past spring she'd been introduced to Betty when we all met up at Baker's Keyboard Lounge. She also knew my friend Hep. Hep Cat Martin owned a filling station and auto repair shop here in the city. I'd known him and his wife, Irma, for a number of years. He played a mean saxophone in a neighborhood band he'd formed when he wasn't working on automobiles. In fact, his involvement in music was how he'd gotten the nickname of "Hep Cat." Surely she'd invited them. Then there was my dear friend, Johnny Delbeck and his wife, Grace. They had a place over in the neighboring city of

Dearborn, but Gran had known Johnny since he was a kid. He and his family had lived next door to her for years, until Johnny and his sisters had grown up. Then his parents sold the house. I'd gotten to know him pretty well when back in 1916 he and his sisters had stayed with Gran for the summer while we were living there, too. He became my closest friend. I thought of Harry Blevins, too. Harry and I had been classmates throughout high school. He'd become an investigative reporter and now worked at the Chicago Tribune, but wouldn't it be grand if he and his wife, Myra, could be at tonight's party? I'd love to see them again.

Turning the corner, I spied Hank's Stop and Shop, a small neighborhood store a couple of blocks away from the house. I pulled up to the curb and parked, thinking I'd pick up a few things to take home with me. When I entered, a bell jingled to announce my arrival. Hank, a small man of about sixty-five, was standing behind the counter, mopping his forehead with an already dampened handkerchief. His gray hair was thinning on top and his gold wire rimmed glasses kept sliding down the bridge of his nose due to the moisture covering his face. He'd been a very handsome man when younger, but now he was stooped with the oncoming of age. I'd known Hank since I'd been in the eighth grade when he and his wife, Rosie, moved into the area from somewhere in Ohio and opened this business. My friends and I would frequent his store after school, if we had the money to buy penny candy. He looked over at me as I entered.

"Hey, Sam," he said, looking pale and exhausted. "How do you like this heat? It's really gettin' to me."

"Yeah, I'm ready for a break in the weather, but I don't see it happening anytime soon," I answered, and looked around the store. "Where's Rosie?"

"Eh, she went down to her sister's just south of Toledo. I suppose it's just as hot there. She don't take well to this heat, either."

After browsing, my purchases were placed on the counter: two six packs of Coca Cola, a six pack of Champagne Velvet beer for Gran, two packs of Lucky Strike cigarettes, and a fifth of premium scotch—why not? After all, it was my birthday. I paid Hank, wished him a good evening, and then headed out to the car once again.

Less than five minutes later, I rounded the corner onto St. Aubin. My eyes darted down the street. I didn't see any cars that belonged to my friends, but that didn't mean anything. They may have parked around the block to hide the fact that there was going to be a party. I did, however, notice that Helen's car was parked in the driveway.

Helen Foster was my grandmother's oldest and dearest friend. She lived four blocks away on Orleans Street. Her husband, Frank, had passed on a couple of years ago, and when he left this earth, he'd left his wife quite comfortably off. She'd gone out within a month of his death and purchased a brand new automobile. Helen stood about five feet four inches tall, was very slender, and when she moved it was with swift determination. She didn't wear glasses—didn't need them, even at the age of seventy-six. Her hair was kept short and she dyed it a dark brown—too dark for her age and coloring. The woman always delighted in getting under my skin; I didn't know why. I, most times, didn't let her, which got under *her* skin.

I pulled up to the curb right in front of the house and parked, hauled the lone bag of items up to the door, and entered.

"SURPRISE!" the two women shouted.

A smile played across my lips. Gran was sitting on the couch, where she had the vantage point of seeing when I would pull up in the burgundy Chevy. She was wearing nothing but her full slip and undergarments underneath. I could see a faint layer of moisture on her upper chest, face and neck. Ruby Flanagan was short and plump, and wore her short, steel gray hair in smooth waves. Helen was sitting in one of the beige chairs, holding a glass of orange juice with ice cubes floating on top. Undoubtedly, she'd added vodka to her juice; something she had become accustomed to doing within the past six months. My grandmother's friend wore a sleeveless light blue dress and had the skirt of it hiked up, exposing her thighs, in an attempt to cool off from the heat and humidity. They both had on party hats, the type that were made from cardboard and came to a point at the top. The hats were fastened under their chins by a string of elastic. No one else was in the living room.

"Well, this is a shock," I said in mock surprise.

My grandmother smiled widely. "I knew it would be, dear." And then she giggled like a school girl.

Moving toward the back of the house, I anticipated another shout from others, but saw no one in the dining room as I passed through. The kitchen was vacant of people, too. I sighed with disappointment and put the bottles of soda and beer into the icebox. So this was it. I was to spend my fortieth birthday with my grandmother–whom I spent most everyday with–and her friend, Helen. Suddenly, I wanted to gather my car keys again and drive over to The Double Shot, a neighborhood bar on the corner of E. Lantz Avenue and Dequindre Street. I didn't dare disappoint the ladies, though.

On top of the kitchen table were stacked four dinner plates with forks and knives sitting in the middle of the top one. Next to those was a platter of last night's leftover fried chicken, cold. I turned when Gran and Helen joined me in the room.

"Why four plates?" I asked.

"Oh," Gran said. "I thought your friend might come home with you."

I smiled. "No, he had other plans."

"Helen and I thought it might be good to go out back and sit at the picnic table under the tree to eat dinner. Maybe it will be cooler."

I nodded. "Sure, whatever you want, Gran. But don't you think you should get some clothes on first?"

****

Dinner was good. We ate the cold chicken from last night, potato salad that Helen had brought with her, and green beans that Gran had heated. I was surprised to see a chocolate cake placed on the picnic table as well. Coffee with the cake would've been good, but it was too hot for that. Instead, we ate the sweet treat with our drinks. Helen sipped at her doctored orange juice while Gran had a bottle of beer in front of her. I was enjoying my smooth scotch from a short glass. As I leaned back and patted my now full stomach, I caught movement at the chain link fence that divided our yard from the neighbor's yard next door. Bobby, a young boy of eight years old, was standing with his face pressed into the fence while his fingers curled around the metal. Albie, Bobby's older brother by four years, was drenching his head in the cold water that gushed from their garden hose at the rear of their house. The younger boy wasn't what you would call a talker. I'd hardly heard him utter ten whole sentences since I'd known him. I waved to the boy and he surprised me by calling through the fence.

"Is that chocolate cake ya got there?"

I nodded. "It sure is. It's delicious, too," I answered him as I watched his brother turn off the hose and shake his head violently, spraying droplets of water from his hair.

Albie joined him at the fence. Looking at Bobby, he yelled loudly enough so we all could hear. "Hey, that ain't polite! You hafta wait to be invited first!"

I smiled and waved to Albie, saying nothing. The boys continued to stare at us.

"Oh, Sam, stop it!" my grandmother said. "Don't tease those boys." She turned to the youngsters. "Well, come on over and you can have some cake. We're celebrating Mr. Flanagan's birthday today."

Bobby didn't need to be asked twice. He hopped the fence in a flash while his brother said, "Is that right? How old are ya today, Mr. Flanagan?"

"Twenty-six," I answered him.

My grandmother slapped me on the arm. "Oh, you," she said. Then turning to the boys, she said "He is not. He's forty today."

"Wow!" Bobby responded.

"Didn't think anyone could live that long, did you?" I asked him, and laughed as he shook his head in astonishment.

"I'll be over in a minute," Albie called. "I gotta do somethin' first."

I watched as the boy ran toward his house and entered the back screen door, allowing it to slam shut after him. Gran and Helen took our dirty dishes and headed inside with them.

"We need to get you boys a plate," Gran said.

I turned my attention back to the younger boy and studied him as he stared at the cake. He sat at the picnic table with his chin resting on his folded arms, his legs swinging back and forth underneath, his eyes never veering from the chocolate confection. He truly was an adorable boy with his light brown hair streaked with blond. His brown eyes, which rested behind tortoise shell glasses, reminded me of an innocent fawn. I often thought of the passing of time, in which these boys would grow older, with sadness–if life could only stay this safe and comforting for them. But it wouldn't stay that way and I knew it. The world at this very moment was torn apart by war half a globe away, but yet affecting our everyday lives here at home. How I hoped and prayed that all the chaos would be over by the time these two reached the age of induction.

I sighed and took another sip of my scotch. I heard the gate clang and looked back to see Albie enter the yard. He was carrying something flat wrapped in old newspaper. His wet hair was combed straight back away from his face, the dampness making its medium brown color appear darker. He was barefoot, like his brother, and wore old cut off pants that rested a couple of inches above his knees, which were fastened at the waist with rope used as a belt. Like his brother, he wore no shirt.

Gran and Helen emerged from the house, carrying two plates, two forks, and two tall glasses of milk. Albie set his mysterious package before me when he reached the picnic table.

"Here ya go, Mr. Flanagan! Bobby and me got ya somethin'," he said.

"Well, you knew all along that it was my birthday, huh?" I teased him.

"Uh, yeah–yeah, we sure did," he lied.

"We *did*?" Bobby asked, scrunching up his nose while looking at his older sibling.

"*Shut up*!" Albie responded. "Ya little jerk!"

I opened the gift after the kids began to eat their cake and pulled out a comic book...*Barney Google and Snuffy Smith.* I held it up for Gran and Helen to see, and I smiled.

"Do ya like it, Mr. Flanagan?" Albie asked.

"I sure do!"

"Well...uh...I was thinkin'," he continued. "Now, if you don't have any place to put that after ya read it, me and Bobby can always keep it with our collection, if ya want. I mean, it'd still be yours, but it'd be in a safe place then."

"But it would still be mine? I could have it anytime I wanted it?"

"Well...yeah," he said hesitantly, while Bobby jerked his head to the side to look at Albie with an expression of "are you nuts?" on his face.

I smiled and agreed to them "storing" the comic book for me. There were times when I really enjoyed these two kids.

Gran slapped Helen on the forearm and told her to run inside and get the gifts they'd gotten for me.

"Why don't you go?" Helen responded.

"'Cause I'm too hot. You do it."

"You're no hotter than I am, ya old fool," Helen shot back. But, in the end, it was she who returned to the house through the kitchen door. When she came out, she carried two gifts; one very small, and one large and rectangular. Both were wrapped in the same white tissue paper, no bows on either.

"Open mine first, Sam," Gran said. "It's the bigger one."

I whistled when I tore through the wrapping and opened the box. "Wow, this is nice," I said, and held it up.

It was a soft beige short sleeved shirt made of cotton percale, and I really liked it. The price tag was still on it and I turned it over to read it—one dollar and fifteen cents.

"Where'd you get the money for this?" I asked Gran, surprised.

She snickered. "I took some of your stash out of your top drawer and had Helen take me to Kerns Department Store," she said.

"Why, you little devil, you! I love it, Gran. Thank you." I rose and went over to her, laying a kiss on her cheek.

Kerns was a department store started by Ernst Kerns back in the early 1880's, and was still standing today on Woodward Avenue. It didn't sit far from the J. L. Hudson store, and I'd gotten a couple of suits there throughout the years. I sat down once again, and Helen handed me her gift.

"And this is from me," she said with a smirk, sliding the very small item across the table to me.

"Oh, Helen, you shouldn't have."

The boys were quiet as I unwrapped it, still filling themselves with chocolate cake. Bobby had a good amount of icing hanging on the corners of his mouth. As soon as they saw what Helen's gift was, Bobby let out an "*oooh*" and Albie started to laugh while he smacked the top of the wooden table with his opened palm. I looked up at Helen and saw that her smirk was even more pronounced.

"Oh Helen! This is terrific! Thank you so much! Do you know how long I've dreamed of having one of these?"

The corners of her mouth began to droop, her forehead creased between the eyebrows, and her eyes narrowed as I continued.

"This is going to make things so much easier for me. All the best detectives in Detroit have one of these, and now I can compete."

"What is it, dear?" Gran asked.

"Gran, it's a decoder pin. Helen found this in a box of Cracker Jack's, I bet, but she doesn't realize what a gem she's found. Good old Captain Jack and Bingo," I said.

"How does it work, dear?"

"Well, see this? You turn it and spell out your clues to a case, and you have to have at least two clues to enter. You wait a few minutes and it tells you who the culprit is."

I eyed Albie, who was covering his mouth with his hand in an attempt to keep from bursting out with laughter. Helen continued to stare at me, trying to figure out whether I was on the up and up with this one. If I was being serious, she didn't like it one bit—the scowl on her face attested to that.

"Oh my goodness," Gran said. "Now you can solve cases in no time." She turned to Helen. "What a wonderful gift you gave him."

****

When the boys left, which was close to half past seven, Helen had gone, too. As Bobby passed me, heading to the gate, I slipped him the plastic decoder pin and put a forefinger to my lips. It would be our secret. His face took on a glow of excitement and he darted out of the yard and to his own home to inspect it.

Gran now lay on the couch, snoring loudly. She was back in her slip and lying in front of the opened windows that allowed no breeze to come through. The sweltering heat overtook her desire to listen to one of her favorite radio broadcasts, *The Adventures of Dick Cole*. I, on the other hand, sat in the beige chair across from her and listened to the thirty minute show. When it was over, I quietly moved into the bathroom off the kitchen and washed up and brushed my teeth. I put on a fresh shirt from my closet and grabbed my hat. It was 8:15 and I was going out, leaving my grandmother to her dreams. I thought I'd head on over to The Double Shot for that drink. It was only a few blocks away and I decided to walk, since I was low on gasoline in the Chevy. I still had time to make a night of it, and I should—after all, it was my fortieth birthday.

Chapter Three

It was early when I woke Saturday morning. I moved through the house quietly so I wouldn't wake Gran. She was still in the position I'd left her in last night; sleeping for twelve hours. I put on a pot of coffee and then moved to the bathroom for a quick shower. Humming a tune, I made toast when I was done. I set two cups of the beverage on a tray—Gran's with cream and mine black—and slathered the toast with peanut butter and grape jelly. I set the toast on a plate, added the plate to the tray, and headed toward the living room. Gran hadn't moved, but her eyes were open.

"Good morning, sleepyhead," I greeted her.

"Good morning," she said with a dry, thick tongue. "What time is it?"

"Going on seven thirty," I told her.

"Did you go somewhere last night?" she asked, sitting up. "I woke about ten o'clock to use the bathroom, but the house was all dark and you weren't here."

I told her where I'd gone. Last night, when I'd arrived at The Double Shot, I'd taken a seat at the bar after putting some coins in the jukebox. I wanted to hear some Jimmy and Tommy Dorsey, some Glenn Miller, and some Count Basie. I had no sooner gotten my drink from Neamon, one of the owners, when a forty-something woman sat next to me, striking up a conversation. She'd already been half in the bag and was eager to rant about the government, telling me she didn't much care for "that man in the White House." I sat politely, but resentfully, listening to her. She'd been ruining the last chance I had to really enjoy my birthday. Finally, when she excused herself to use the ladies room, I paid Neamon for my two drinks and high-tailed it out of there. I arrived home shortly before eleven o'clock, finding Gran still sleeping on the sofa.

Even though it was only seven thirty in the morning, the temperature seemed to be nearing eighty degrees. For that reason, I'd put on the new short sleeved shirt Gran had given me yesterday with a pair of brown trousers. I left the shirt opened a couple of buttons at the neck, hoping to keep a bit cooler.

"You're going into the office?" Gran asked, as she picked up a slice of toast. "Are you working on a case?"

"I don't have a case, but I'm going into the office today. I need to be there if someone does need to hire a detective. What are your plans?"

"Helen and I were going to go to the victory garden on the corner a couple of blocks over, but I'm not sure I want to walk in this heat to meet her. This heat makes me feel weak," she said.

"No, Gran. You're not going anywhere. Stay out of the sun," I cautioned her. "I don't want you passing out."

But she just nodded as she sipped at her coffee.

****

I parked the car, and on the way into the office, I stopped to buy a newspaper from Hooch Beasle, whose newsstand was on the corner.

Hooch Beasle was a kid of sixteen who should've been attending school throughout the little more than nine months it was in session, but he wasn't. A couple of years ago, he'd gotten caught for the second time by the authorities making homemade moonshine in an outbuilding that sat at the rear of the property that his mother's house sat on. His father had died the year before, and he was trying to make money that he, his mother, and his younger siblings—a sister and three brothers—needed to survive. When caught the first time, the judge slapped him on the wrist by putting the fear of God into him. Apparently, it didn't stick because he got caught a second time. This time, he wasn't so lucky as to have the same judge or the same warning. They hauled his rear off to juvenile detention for three months. It nearly killed his mother by breaking her heart, and when he was released, he vowed never to go outside of the law again; if for nothing else, for his love and concern for her. Hence, the nickname "Hooch"—his Christian name was Wallace. Now he had abandoned any type of education for selling newspapers and odds and ends at his little corner stand.

Sitting beside a stack of the Detroit News was a basket filled with fruit. He had a few apples, a few peaches, a pear—and what was this? Hooch had two bananas among the other fruit! My eyes widened. Bananas were almost impossible to get with the food rationing that was taking place.

"Hey, where'd you get those?" I asked him.

"Never you mind, Mr. Flanagan. All you need to know is I got 'em. You interested?"

"Of course," I said. "How much?" I was reaching in my right pants pocket to bring out my change for the paper and the fruit.

"Ten cents a piece," he said.

"What? That's highway robbery!" I objected.

"Take it or leave it," he said with his chin in the air.

I looked at him as if he were nuts. His deep black hair was oily, and the long strands that framed his face were tucked behind his ears. He had the same color of hair that I had, but his eyes were brown, whereas mine were blue. He wouldn't be a bad looking boy if he'd clean up. Staring at him, I was silent, wondering whether it was worth it to try to haggle further over the price.

"You don't want 'em, someone else will," he said.

I brought out a quarter, handing it over to him begrudgingly—twenty cents for the bananas and a nickel for the Detroit News.

"You drive a hard bargain, Hooch."

"That, I do, Mr. Flanagan…that, I do." And with a triumphant smirk, he threw the coin in his wooden bowl under his counter.

****

I reached the second floor of my office building by taking the steps two at a time. Moving past Oliver Treadwell's door, I noticed it was shut. I figured the little guy wasn't in yet. He was a freelance photographer for a couple of city newspapers, and kept a private office here in the building. About to put the key into my own door, I also noticed that the door to the office directly across from mine was wide open. That was odd because that space had been vacant for the last five years or more. I cautiously moved toward it and stuck my head in.

"Hello?" I called out. I saw no one, but it looked as though someone had been there, attempting to wash away the dust, dirt, and grime. Over the back of a battered chair, sitting behind a battered desk, was a brown suit jacket.

"Well, hello," responded a voice from behind me. "And who are you?"

I turned to see a guy I pegged to be in his late twenties, who stood about five feet five inches tall. I towered above him by a good nine inches. His weight was normal for his height. His hair—dark black, like mine and Hooch's—was cut short, parted in the middle, and was plastered to his head with pomade. This guy had a full, black mustache, also waxed, sitting under his nose, but was otherwise clean shaven. Black, horn-rimmed glasses sat across the bridge of his nose. Even under the mustache, I could tell he had a serious overbite. The little man was dressed in a crisp white shirt with a solid brown tie, which matched his trousers. I stepped back, away from the door.

"I have the office across from this one," I said. I nodded back toward the open door. "Are you renting this?"

"Sure am," he said crisply, and he then extended his hand. "Irwin Malcolm Wright, Attorney at Law. I was hoping you were a potential client. So you're the private dick, huh?" he asked, as he nodded toward my door.

"Yeah, Sam Flanagan," I responded, and shook his hand.

"Say, where'd you get those?" He was eying my bananas.

"Kid on the corner."

"Wouldn't see your way fit to selling me one, would you? How much you pay for them?"

I looked lovingly down at the fruit in my hand. "Eh, I don't know. I paid a pretty penny for them, that's for sure. Paid a quarter apiece for them." How was he to know, right? I'd bought the only two that Hooch had.

He whistled. "Wow!" Still, his eyes were on the bananas.

"Tell you what," I said. "I'll let you have one for twenty cents, seeing as how you're going to be my neighbor."

He reached into his pocket and sorted through his change. He forked over a dime and two nickels. "That's swell of you, Flanagan. Appreciate it."

"Don't mention it," I said, heading to unlock my door with a smirk on my face. He called out my name, and I turned to him once again. His hand was outstretched.

"Here are some of my cards. Of course, with my new office here, I'll have to get new ones made up. I was a partner with my father in his law firm. He promised me the position after I graduated from law school, but after six months of him never letting me do anything but bring him coffee and his morning paper, I felt it was time to establish my own practice. When I get my phone hooked up in here, you can jot the number on these and cross off my dad's name. You can pass them out until I can get some new ones made."

I accepted his offering and unlocked my door, shutting it as I entered the small space. Opening my top desk drawer, I threw in the business cards, and proceeded to spend most of the morning gazing out the window onto the people walking along Woodward Avenue, clipping my fingernails, and reading the Detroit News. Finally, not one word was mentioned in the periodical about the riot the city had endured last month. What a mess that had been!

Back on June 20 of this year, a clash between whites and coloreds had broken out over on Belle Isle, the small recreational island that sat off the city in the Detroit river. Tensions had been brewing ever since the beginning of the war, when approximately 350,000 people had migrated from the south to Detroit. Fifty thousand of those, or more, were colored. The "Arsenal of Democracy," as we'd become known, offered jobs in the defense industry, mass producing military hardware, airplanes, tanks, and other vehicles. The mobs began to assault one another, as well as innocent bystanders. Those getting off the streetcars didn't know what they were walking into. Businesses were burned and looted and thirty-five deaths resulted, most of the victims being colored. (Thank God my office was on the second floor of the building.) Finally, Governor Harry Kelly and Mayor Edward Jeffries, Jr. asked the president of the United States to get involved. Roosevelt responded by sending in federal troops and things began to settle down. The whole thing lasted three days. I stayed home from the office after driving over to get Helen, Gran's friend. Making her stay with us for the duration of the unrest, I didn't let either one of them wander outside. The carnage contained itself to the heart of the city, but I couldn't be sure scuffles wouldn't break out in the neighborhood.

Although I had opened the windows before I sat behind my desk this morning, no air was circulating in the small space. I moved to open the door leading to the hall, hoping a breeze would run through, and there was Irwin Malcolm Wright, sitting at his desk, twirling a pencil while eating his banana. I waved as he looked at me and then moved to sit in my seat once again. When I looked out into the hall again, he was still staring. *Oh boy,* I thought, *this might be a problem.* I buried my head behind the newspaper, reading what I'd already read. His voice startled me. I looked over the top of the paper and saw he was standing at the edge of my desk.

"Let me ask you something, Mr. Flanagan," he said.

"Okay, shoot."

"What should I look for in a good secretary? I've interviewed two this morning and they just don't seem to be what I'm looking for."

"Well, what are you looking for?" I asked him.

"Oh, I don't know—an efficient girl, someone who's pleasant and has a nice phone voice."

"Sounds good to me," I said. "What was wrong with the two you interviewed?"

"The first one was pretty but she came in chewing gum, which she cracked, and told me she didn't know how to type very well."

"Ah," I said, nodding my head. "That won't do."

"The other one said she typed sixty words a minute without errors and seemed competent."

"Why didn't you like her?"

"She was on the pudgy side and had a huge mole on the side of her nose. I couldn't take my eyes off the black hair that was growing from it," he admitted. "I'm not sure if that would look good to prospective clients."

"I don't think that has anything to do with it, do you?" I asked. "As long as she's competent."

"I guess you're right," he said, and walked back to his own office without another word.

I went back to hiding behind my newspaper until I heard some motion out in the hall. I glanced up just in time to see a woman of about sixty walking into Irwin's office. She had gray hair which was severely pulled back from her face. Although the temperature outside was above ninety, she wore a lightweight navy blue sweater over her cotton light blue dress. When she responded to the attorney's questions, she did it in an overly loud voice. He looked past the woman and over to me. I slowly shook my head from side to side. He dismissed her and I could see him sigh with disappointment when she was out of sight. Twenty minutes later, another woman, about thirty years younger than the last, knocked softly on his door, causing him to raise his head. She wasn't half bad, with golden blonde hair and a tight green skirt. She sat in the wooden chair facing his desk, and I saw the young man straighten with enthusiasm. Before he could begin the interview, I heard her shooting him questions, one after another. How much will I get paid? Will I be in the courtroom with you? Do I have to make coffee, because I don't know how to make coffee? Will this be my desk?

He looked over at me with a plea of "help" on his face, and I shook my head no. He sent her away.

He rose from his chair and, despite the torrid heat, put his suit jacket on. Irwin placed a brown fedora atop his waxed head and departed from his new office, locking it behind him. The young man came to stand in my doorway.

"It's almost noon, Mr. Flanagan. Time for lunch. Where would you like to go?"

I was caught off guard. I could see that maybe my new neighbor was going to be more of a problem than I would've liked. Straightening in my chair, I cleared my throat.

"Aw, gee, Irwin; I'd love to have lunch with you, but I'm expecting a call. Maybe some other time?"

He nodded his head and turned away, looking dejected. The young attorney wasn't having such a good start and I began to feel sorry for him. I almost rose from my chair to go out and tell him to wait—I'd changed my mind. *Almost*—but I caught myself from making *that* mistake. Instead, I put my feet up on the desk, leaned back in my chair, and fell asleep.

****

When I woke, the side of my new shirt had a spot of dampness from where I'd drooled. I sat up, wiping the corner of my mouth, and looked at my watch. It was twenty minutes after two o'clock. My door leading to the hall was still wide open and when I glanced toward the newly inhabited office space, I didn't see the little guy, but his door was wide open, too. That call that I'd lied about to Irwin never came through. No calls had come through at all today, so I thought I may as well call it a day and go home. Rising from my desk, I turned to close the windows. Glancing down onto the street, I saw

Irwin racing to the building. He quickly appeared in my doorway, holding up another banana.

"Guess where I got this?" he asked, out of breath.

I felt my body fill with heat and wondered if my face and neck had turned red. If he got that from Hooch's stand—and where else *could* he have gotten it? —I had been found out. He'd probably now demand I reimburse him his ten cents.

"Uh, where?" I asked him, nervously.

"That kid on the corner," he beamed. "And guess what I told him? I just picked up the banana and before he could tell me it would be a quarter, I told him I was paying twenty cents for the banana and wouldn't pay anything else. He didn't even argue with me. He just looked at me sort of strange and took my money." He hesitated in his story and smiled widely. "You really need to get a backbone, Flanagan, and not let people make a fool out of you."

"You're amazing, Irwin!" I said to him, and he turned and entered his office, feeling extremely proud of himself. He shut the door.

I moved out into the hall and locked my own door. It was only two thirty in the afternoon, but I couldn't take the inactivity and I couldn't take the heat. I was going to go home to undress and lie on my bed.

Moving toward the stairs, I noticed a woman round the corner and come toward me in the hall. She stood about five feet four inches tall, and it looked as though it wouldn't hurt her to gain ten or twenty pounds. She had jet black hair that was pulled back and tied at the base of her neck with a white ribbon, and had on a thinly worn green housedress. She passed me and seemed to be looking for an office she'd never been to before, moving her head from side to side to check out the names and numbers on the doors. Undoubtedly, she was to be interviewed next by Irwin. He'd have to make the decision about this one all on his own.

When she came to my door, she stopped, looked at a piece of paper she was holding, and looked up again. The woman then knocked.

"He's not there," I called back to her.

Before I could tell her that *I* was Sam Flanagan, she fell against the door jamb to my office, covered her face with both hands, and broke out into heavy tears.

CHAPTER FOUR

Quickly, I approached her and placed my hand on her shoulder.

"Hey, what's wrong?"

"You don't understand," she moaned. "I have nowhere else to turn. He was my last hope."

I let out a little laugh and said, "It's all right. You didn't give me a chance to tell you that I am he. I'm Sam Flanagan."

She looked up and wiped under her nose and then used the ball of her palm to brush the tears from her eyes.

"You're him? You're the detective?"

"I've got this to prove it," I said, holding up the key to my office for her to see. And then I unlocked the door and ushered her in.

She sat in the chair facing my desk while I sat on the edge of it, facing her. Like her clothing, she looked old beyond her years. Her dark brown eyes were blood shot and puffy. This hadn't been the first time she'd cried today. I passed her the box of tissues that sat near me and she grabbed one, and then blew her nose. I waited until she was calm.

"Feeling a bit better?" I asked her.

She nodded and then swiped a clean tissue under her nose again. She sighed and leaned back in the chair, looking exhausted. I moved around and sat in my own chair, resting my elbows on the wooden surface of my desk.

"You wanted to see me about something? Just take your time and tell me about your situation."

She cleared her throat and began by telling me that when she was seventeen, she and her brother had made their way to the United States by ocean liner. The previous year, her parents had died and she no longer felt an obligation to stay in her home town of Librizzi, Sicily, which she felt held nothing for her in the way of a future. This was back in 1922, and two months after arriving in the United States, she had word from her uncle that his godson, Carlo, was also coming to Detroit. He wanted her to befriend the young man and show him the city. Within five months of his arrival, they were married.

"He was twenty-nine at the time, twelve years older than myself," she said. "But he was so good to Nito and me." She raised her eyes and looked at me. "Nito…that's my brother. He was fourteen at the time."

Studying her as she spoke, I could well imagine what a beauty she had been when she was younger. This woman had a sense of femininity and delicateness about her…a sweet softness.

"This is very interesting…uh…."

"Sophia…Sophia Anders," she stated.

"Well, Mrs. Anders, how is it that I can help you?"

She inhaled deeply and then slowly her breath came whooshing out. She straightened in her chair, and with a voice that was much stronger, she told me what she'd really come for.

"I want you to clear my husband of the charge of murder," Sophia Anders said.

I stared at her for a moment. "Does he have a lawyer, Mrs. Anders?"

"No, you don't understand. This happened years ago and he's been serving time in the state penitentiary for almost nineteen years. You see, when Carlo was charged with this crime, I had just found out I was pregnant. We have a son, Carlo Jr., who will turn nineteen this coming November. The boy was born months after his father had gone to prison. He never really knew Carlo in the normal sense. It's for him. I want you to clear his father's name for him. He's recently been seeing a girl…a lovely girl, Mr. Flanagan. She comes from a good home and good people. I want him to be able to take his name back. I want *my* name back again." She paused and took in air. "You see, my husband was killed in prison nine months ago. He's gone, but we can clear his name, if only you'll help."

Staring at the woman, I squinted with my eyes and felt an uncomfortable twinge crawl up my spine. Something stirred within me. Something wasn't right here.

"Tell me what your true married name is," I asked.

"Andolucci…my husband was Carlo Andolucci."

Andolucci…I stood slowly, even though my knees felt like rubber. Leaning on the desk, I moved closer toward her. I went all hot inside, and it had nothing to do with the high temperature and humidity in the room.

"I'm sorry, but I'm working on a case right now. I can't help you," I lied.

"Oh, but please…."

I held up my hand, cutting her off.

"There's nothing I can do. Now if you'll excuse me," I said as I came out from behind my desk and passed her, opening the door leading to the hall. "Good day, Mrs. Andolucci."

She turned in her chair, making one more plea. "He didn't do it, Mr. Flanagan. I know that as sure as I'm sitting here. He didn't do it! He was with me at the time those people were killed!"

"Good day, Mrs. Andolucci."

****

As I stared down onto Woodward Avenue from my second story office, I saw her about to climb aboard the trolley. Before she stepped up, she turned and looked my way. There was pain and sadness on her face and I could tell the tears had returned. I had nothing personally against this woman, but she was the victim of circumstance. There was no way I was going to help her.

I continued to watch the street below until the trolley had gone from my vision. My hat was resting on the top of my filing cabinet and I reached to the right to retrieve it. Turning around to make my exit, I saw a young woman lowering herself into the chair facing my desk...the chair that Mrs. Sophia Andolucci had vacated just moments before. Her presence startled me and an involuntary grunt escaped from my throat. She looked up when she heard it.

"You were just leaving, weren't you?" she asked in a soft and feminine, but out of breath voice.

"Actually, I was."

"Well; then, I'm glad I caught you. I meant to be here earlier; really I did, but I'm moving and the apartment is still such a mess. Oh my lord, what a chore it is to move to a new place! I mean, you don't realize *everything* you've accumulated and then you have to pack it all, move it, and then *unpack* it all...but I'm just rattling on! I guess I'm a bit nervous, actually. I guess what I mean to say, though, is that it will be extremely convenient. I moved to an apartment just around the corner...on W. Hancock Street. Just above the little bakery there. Have you ever been there? To the bakery, I mean. They have the most delicious small strawberry cakes!"

"Uh…Missus...?"

"Kirkendahl…Frances Kirkendahl. But *please* don't call me Frances. I hate that! Why my mother ever named me Frances, I'll never know. Thank God my father had the sense to start calling me Frankie when I was a little girl! Call me that. Call me Frankie."

She stopped and looked up at me to where I still stood, holding my hat.

"Well? Shouldn't you be writing any of this down?"

I sighed, replaced my hat on the filing cabinet, and sat opposite her at my desk.

"Don't worry, Mrs. Kirkendahl. I think I can remember everything you've said so far."

I studied her. She was very cute. Frankie Kirkendahl weighed no more than one hundred and twenty pounds in her five foot five inch petite frame. The young woman wore a dark green skirt that hugged her hips and thighs with a short-sleeved pale tan blouse that was tied at the base of her neck with a huge, floppy bow. Her hair was rolled away from her face, caught up above each ear with a large green barrette, while the back fell in soft curls past her shoulders. It was deep reddish brown and she stared at me with lovely dark brown eyes. Faded freckles spanned her cute up-turned nose and spread out across her cheeks.

"First of all," she continued. "I'm not married, so I'm not a 'Missus.' And, secondly, I told you to call me Frankie."

"Okay, Frankie," I said. "Why don't you begin by telling me why you're here?"

She slumped back in the chair, dejectedly. "*Oh no*!" she wailed. "Have you hired someone?"

I looked around my small office. When my eyes met hers again, I said, "No…no, it's just me here."

That tidbit of information seemed to rejuvenate her. She bolted upright with a sigh of relief. Frankie folded her hands in her lap and said, "Thank goodness! Okay, then shoot!"

"Shoot?"

Confusion must've shown on my face. What *was* this? Did she need to hire a detective or not? Was this going to be a game of twenty questions until I finally got the exact nature of the case out of her? I really wasn't in the mood for games. Her expression was one of surprise that I could be so clueless.

"Well, ask me something," she demanded.

"Listen…uh…Frankie; I'm really not in the right frame of mind for all of this, so why don't you just tell me what you think I need to know."

I leaned back in my chair, placing my right ankle on top of my left knee. My hands came together in front of me, and I intertwined my fingers as I rested my elbows on the arms of my chair. She stared at me in amazement.

"You sure have a strange way of doing things. Well, okay…here goes. As I told you before, I'm Frankie Kirkendahl. I'm twenty-nine years old and live right around the corner now, so that will be convenient if you ever need me at a moment's notice," she said breathlessly.

My eyebrows came together in confusion once again. Whether she noticed my expression or not, she didn't hesitate, but plowed right along.

"I'm usually very punctual and I get along quite well with people. I type about forty-eight words per minute, but what I lack in speed I make up for with accuracy. I don't make mistakes, and on the rare occasion I do make one, I find it and correct it. I'm a whiz at finding things out, so if you ever need me for research…."

She went on talking and I stopped listening and smiled at her. It dawned on me that Miss Frankie Kirkendahl had meandered into the wrong office. She didn't need a private investigator—she needed a job! This was Irwin Malcolm Wright's next candidate for a secretary.

As if on cue, I saw the little guy out in the hall, heading toward my office. When he stepped inside, he caught sight of the young lady, and she stopped speaking.

"Oh," he said in embarrassment. "I'm sorry, Mr. Flanagan. I didn't know you were with a client."

"*You're not* Mr. Wright?" she asked in surprise, while pointing a red nail-tipped index finger my way.

"Irwin Malcolm Wright, meet Miss Frankie Kirkendahl," I said.

"Frankie?" He was bewildered, looking from me to the woman and back to me again.

"That's right. Her name is actually Frances, but don't call her that—she hates being called that. Call her Frankie. She's come to see you about a job, Irwin." And then I looked her way. "It seems you've wandered into the wrong office, Miss Kirkendahl. If you ever need a private detective though, I'll still be here."

She jumped up from where she'd been sitting as if hot coals had been deposited in her lap. A look of anger formed on her face.

"Well! Of all the nerve! And you just let me go on and on and on," she spit while facing me. She gave a grunt while raising her chin in the air, turned on her heels, and walked out into the hall. Before following her, Irwin turned to me with the expression of "Well, what do you think?" I gave him the thumbs up sign.

CHAPTER FIVE

In front of the house on St. Aubin, I parked the auto at the curb. The sun beat down with a vengeance, as if trying to cook everything under its rays. Entering the small foyer, I was met with silence. Gran wasn't in the front parlor, and as I moved toward the kitchen in the back, I found the place empty. I hoped she hadn't gone against my wishes and walked to meet Helen to pick vegetables from the neighborhood garden.

In the kitchen, I found Shamus the kitten sitting on the sill of the window, moving his tail lazily and gazing out into the summer sunshine. We'd acquired him a couple of months ago when he came knocking at our door in the middle of a thunderstorm. I heard his knock and graciously offered him shelter for the night and he'd never left. He heard my movement and turned his soft, gray face toward me, meowing twice before resuming his study of something outside which held his attention. The side window faced Albie and Bobby's house and I heard yelps of laughter coming from their backyard. I moved closer and lowered my head to see what was going on. There was Gran, sitting in a lawn chair next to the boys' mother. The two women were laughing with delight as the kids had hold of the garden hose, spraying water at them. I couldn't help but smile when I heard my grandmother say, "Here, Bobby, spray it right in my face." I longed to be cool, too, but instead of joining them, I moved to my bedroom and removed my clothing. Keeping only my cotton boxer shorts on, I pulled the bedspread down completely and lay with only the top sheet covering me from the waist down. It didn't seem to be a remedy for this heat. Feeling drained, I allowed myself to slip into a deep sleep.

****

"Sam? Sam, get up and eat something."

Prying my eyes open, I saw Gran standing in the doorway of my room. The sun was going down and I actually felt a small breeze entering the house from my window.

"Huh?" I said, still not fully awake.

"I ate a couple of hours ago. You need to get up and eat something," she said again.

"I'm all right, Gran. I'll eat later."

"Well, okay then. There's egg salad in the icebox when you're ready, dear."

My grandmother backed away from my door and my head hit the pillow once again. My world went dark with slumber.

I don't know how long I'd slept, but it was dark outside when I heard my name being called out, rousing me from sleep for a second time.

"*What? What is it?*" I said in a startled voice. Propping myself up on my elbows, I felt my heart beating uncomfortably fast within my chest.

"Sam, get up. *Inner Sanctum* is coming on," my grandmother said.

Allowing myself to lay back on my pillow, I breathed easier. My heart rate was returning to normal, now realizing it was only Gran.

"Nah, you go ahead and listen to it. I don't feel like getting up."

"Oh come on, sleepyhead. You love that show!"

"No, Gran, please. I'd rather go back to sleep," I told her.

Instead of taking my protests seriously, my grandmother came farther into my room and stood at the side of my bed. She reached out and started to tickle the sides of my stomach while saying, "Come on and get up. I'll fix you a sandwich to eat while we listen to the program."

I pushed her hands away and sighed loudly. "Stop it! I don't want to get up. You go listen to it if you want."

"But I'll get scared if I have to listen alone. Are you feeling all right? You're not coming down with anything, are you?"

"No, it's just the heat. I'm tired, that's all."

She began to tickle me once again and I got angry. I shoved her hands away more forcefully and yelled, "*Leave me alone*! *Just go now*!"

My grandmother straightened, and even in the dimness of the room, I could see the look of hurt on her face. She backed away without another word, shutting the door as she left. I closed my eyes and sighed loudly when she was gone. I was angry at her for pestering me and I was angry at myself for the way I'd reacted. Of course, I knew what I was *really* doing. Sleeping the day and evening away was my escape. If I fell into a deep sleep, I wouldn't have to think. The last thing I wanted to do was to think of Carlo Andolucci and how he'd devastated my family almost twenty years ago.

CHAPTER SIX

When I woke, it was on my own this time, and the clock read a quarter after three in the morning. I couldn't believe I'd been dead to the world for that period of time–about twelve hours!

In the bathroom, I splashed cold water on my face to rinse away the grogginess. I felt like garbage, my mind seeming to be in fragments. It was as if I couldn't fully wake up or focus. I sat on the toilet with the lid down and laid a cold, wet washcloth on the back of my neck.

Shamus entered the room and went to his litter box, ignoring my presence, and then left without a sideways glance at me when he'd finished his business. I sat there maybe another ten minutes, staring at the floor with my elbows resting on the tops of my thighs. Gran's pained expression when I'd yelled at her earlier was playing over and over in my mind. An uncomfortable guilt ran through my body, burrowing itself deep into my soul. I shouldn't have done it–not to Gran. Thinking back, I couldn't remember one time when she'd yelled at me or had a cross word for me...not when I was a boy, and not as a man. Even though I paid the bills now, it was still her house and she'd graciously offered me a home here when I needed shelter the most. If anyone was deserving of decent treatment, it was her.

I sighed heavily and ran the cold cloth over my face once again before rising to enter the kitchen. I was hungry. After making two egg salad sandwiches and pouring a large glass of milk, I sat down at the kitchen table to eat and watched Shamus, who was now keeping watch at his perch on the window sill. He pulled his light blue eyes away from the darkness outside and scrutinized me.

"Well, what are *you* looking at?" I muttered. Without making a sound, he turned back to view the night.

It was only when I was finished and was heading for my room to get my cigarettes and matches off of my chest of drawers, that I noticed my grandmother's bedroom door was standing wide open as I passed. I stopped and turned my gaze toward the interior of her room, trying to adjust my vision to the utter darkness within. It was strange that she hadn't shut her door tonight as she always did. Maybe she felt the heat was too much to have the room closed up. I didn't hear any snoring, soft or otherwise, coming from the interior. Imagining her lying in her bed, awake and staring at me standing at her doorway, I called to her softly.

"Gran, are you awake?"

There was no response. I didn't blame her. I wouldn't have wanted to talk to me, either…not after I'd treated her the way I did earlier this evening. I called out again in a slightly louder tone.

"Gran? May I come in? I'm very sorry about what happened tonight. I don't know what got into me."

Of course, I *did* know what had gotten into me to cause me to lash out. Mrs. Sophia Andolucci's visit to my office had put me in a foul mood. Her visit brought up painful memories that I didn't want to face again—didn't want to be reminded of. It was awkward enough for *me* to relive; how could I explain it to Gran? I didn't want to hurt *her* by bringing it up, but instead, I'd hurt her deeply anyway. Instead of explaining to her what I was feeling and why I was feeling the way I was, I'd taken it out on my grandmother.

I waited some seconds for her to respond, thinking she just might be sleeping after all, but I suddenly realized that I not only didn't hear any snoring emanating from her, I didn't hear any soft breathing, either. A slight wave of panic ran through me.

"Hey, Gran?" I said, a bit louder. No answer—no nothing.

Moving into the room quietly, I felt my way along the wall until I came to the foot of her bed. I put my hand down and began to feel the surface and couldn't find her feet. My hand edged up toward the middle and I felt nothing...I felt no one. That's when I turned to the wall near the door and flipped on the light switch. Glancing back at the bed, I saw she wasn't there. *What in the world...?* It was past 3:30 in the morning and my grandmother wasn't in her bed—hadn't *been* in her bed. It was still made; the covers hadn't been lowered.

Quickly, I moved to the front parlor and trained my eyes on the sofa. From the moonlight streaming in through the picture window, I could see that my grandmother wasn't lying on it. My gaze landed on the front door, but it was closed. Moving forward, I opened it and looked out onto the porch. She wasn't there, either. What had happened? Where had she gone? Where could she be? Of course, I had a nagging feeling of what had happened...I'd yelled at her and she left. Was that how it went? How could it be anything else? My grandmother had run...but she'd run to *where*?

I turned on the small lamp that sat on the end table near the chair, and then went to my bedroom to get my cigarettes and pack of matches. When I returned, I sat down and moved the ashtray that was sitting on the end table to the arm of the chair. Lighting a Lucky Strike, I inhaled deeply and tried to think of where Gran would have run to. Only two logical places came to mind…next door—to where she had been earlier when I'd arrived home—or to Helen's, her best friend. It seemed to me that it would be more likely that she would call Helen. I'd find out for sure when the sun came up. I certainly couldn't call the woman's home at this hour. There was nothing I could do now; I'd just have to wait. I would call Helen's and talk to my grandmother, apologizing for my rotten behavior, hoping she could forgive me. But I *wouldn't* tell her about Sophia Andolucci. I didn't want the memories of that night almost twenty years ago to upset her, too.

Now that I had been forced to recall those agonizing events, it felt as though they had occurred just yesterday….

****

It was Thursday, April 24, 1924 and the day was going well. Andy Gunnarson, my good friend from high school, and I were planning to practice his pitching in his backyard later that afternoon. Andy was tall and lanky with fair skin and almost whitish blond hair, carrying with him all the traits of his Swedish ancestors. He had a talent on the baseball field, and the University of Detroit had recognized this, making him their starting pitcher for the team in the second semester of his freshman year, and ever since. He'd played in high school, too; where I had met him, and where he had come to be known as "Bullet Gunnarson", partly because of "Gun" in his name, but mostly because he could pitch a ball faster than any of us had ever seen. When he enrolled in college and joined the University of Detroit team, the name had stuck. A couple of days before, his coach had called him into the office, telling him a few scouts would be watching him during the game on this upcoming Monday, and that he should be prepared and look sharp. I was going to go over and help him practice by catching his pitches.

He wanted to be a teacher and his family was fortunate enough to have the means to send him to college in pursuit of that goal. He came from a long line of Catholics and the University of Detroit was the only school his parents would consider sending him to. Of course, *my* parents had reservations about our friendship because of his Catholic background, even though he was an all around nice guy. But what could they really say? I was going to be twenty-one that summer and felt I could now choose my own friends.

It was going on four o'clock, the time we'd agreed to meet. My father caught me at the kitchen sink, getting a drink of water.

"I'm taking your mother out for dinner. I'd like you to cut the grass while we're gone," he said.

I set my glass down on the counter and looked at him. He was dressed in a black suit with white shirt and a silver tie around his neck. Connor Flanagan was a bit over six feet tall and handsome in a rugged way. His chin appeared chiseled—squared off in shape, with a deep cleft in it. I'd gotten my black hair and light blue eyes from him. Today he was looking extremely keen.

"Wow, what's the occasion?"

"Your mother and I have been married twenty-five years today," he said, smiling. "I'm taking her to that Italian place she's always wanted to go to, but don't tell her. She doesn't know where we're going."

I whistled and said, "Nice, Dad. You sure look sharp. But I'll cut the grass when I get home from Andy's."

"No, son, I'm asking you to cut it before you go. We're supposed to get some rain this evening."

"I can't, Dad. Andy's expecting me in about ten minutes. He needs to practice his pitching. I'll do it when I get home."

He looked sternly at me and pointed his finger just inches from my face. "Sam, I am telling you to do something, and I expect you to do what you're told."

I slapped his hand away and yelled, "I'm not a little kid anymore. I don't see what the big deal is! I'll do it later." I then ran out the back door, letting it slam as I climbed on my bike and pedaled down the driveway and out onto the street. I'd heard him yell my name from the front door, but I never turned around and I never answered him.

We'd been in Andy's back yard for just over two hours when his mother stuck her head out the door, saying my sister, Eva, had called, telling me to come home, that my grandparents were coming over.

"It must be something important, Sam. She said your grandfather told her to get you home right away," she called out.

I thanked her for the message and told Andy to throw just a few more pitches. But those few pitches turned into a few more, and then a few more after that. Suddenly, Andy stopped throwing the ball and his eyes focused behind me and to the right. I heard a gate opening and turned, following his gaze. My grandfather was entering the yard and heading for me.

"Did your sister call to tell you to get your butt home?" he asked sternly in his Irish brogue.

"Yeah, I guess time got away from me. What's up?"

"Get in the car!" he almost yelled.

"I can't. I've got my bike."

My grandfather came closer, grabbing my left ear with his right hand. He started to pull me toward the gate.

"Hey!" I called out in protest, partly because he was hurting me, but mostly because I was feeling an extreme embarrassment in front of Andy. I tried to brush his hand from my ear, but he held on tight and didn't release me until we got to the car, in which Gran and Eva sat. As I climbed in next to my sister in the back seat, I heard Andy call from the gate, "I'll bring your bike home to you tomorrow!"

Once inside, I turned to my sister while rubbing my ear. "Where we going?"

"I don't know," she said.

Twenty minutes later, we were turning into the parking lot at Harper Hospital in the heart of the city. I was confused. Why were we here? What happened?

About four police cars had been parked near the emergency entrance. Inside, doctors and nurses were running from one room to another. Police were talking to a young man in one corner of the lobby. He looked to be in his twenties and was cradling his left arm in a towel that used to be white, but was now turning red from blood. He answered their questions in excited broken English. I tried to make out what the young foreigner was saying as my grandfather moved to the information desk, but couldn't understand. When he returned to us, my grandfather gestured to a group of chairs lining one wall. We sat down and I finally leaned forward, looking past Eva and Gran, and asked, "What in the world is going on? Why are we here?"

My grandfather didn't answer me. Instead, he and my grandmother rose from their seats and began walking toward a doctor who was heading in our direction. I couldn't hear what was being said and I turned to Eva to ask her if she knew anything. She claimed she knew nothing, but told me she didn't like this…she had a bad feeling about being here in the hospital. I looked back at my grandparents and the doctor and saw the medical man shaking his head. Gran's legs seemed to have weakened, because she fell against my grandfather and buried her head in his chest. Her sobs reached my ears and I felt everything inside go numb with fear. I felt so afraid. *What is going on? Why are we here?*

Moments later, my grandparents returned to us and then led us to the hospital cafeteria, where they bought my sister and me a soda and explained to us what they'd learned. My father had taken my mother, his wife of twenty-five years now, to the Italian restaurant she'd always wanted to eat at—La Bella Luna. Part way through their dinner, a man carrying a Tommy gun entered the eating establishment and opened fire. My father dove across the table, knocking my mother to the floor. He covered her with his own body, taking three bullets to the back, but not before my mother was struck in the upper left arm, severing a main artery. At that very moment, my mother was in surgery, where the doctors were trying to repair that artery. She'd lost a great amount of blood, but they felt confident she would survive. My father hadn't been so lucky. The doctor who had spoken to my grandparents told them of my father's death. *My father's death*—I was screaming, crying on the inside, but my outward appearance was blank, numb. All I could think about was the last time I'd seen him. I could only think of the disrespect I'd shown toward him. And now, this. This was entirely my fault. I hadn't obeyed my grandfather and left Andy's right away. If I had, we could've said goodbye to my father. Because of my disrespect and stupidity, precious time had been lost. I could've apologized to him. Instead, he left this earth without hearing me tell him I was sorry for the way I'd behaved. He left without hearing how much I loved him. I prevented my grandparents from seeing their only surviving son before he passed away. How could they ever forgive me for this? As all of this flooded my mind, I watched Eva break down and cry without end, with no expression of my own grief.

That night, it was close to midnight when we left the hospital. Mom was out of surgery, but they wouldn't let us in the recovery room to see her. The doctor finally came out to tell us that she had woken but her arm would never be the same, having now lost movement in it due to the damaged artery. But she was alive and would survive, and that's what was important. When she became aware of her situation, she'd asked about my father. Instead of answering her, they'd injected her with a heavy sedative. She was sleeping now, so we left. My grandfather drove to my grandparents' home and Gran ran in to collect their night clothes. They would stay with us over the next few weeks. Once home, I emerged from my grandfathers' car and looked up into the blackened night sky when I heard a rumbling of thunder. I entered our garage and went to the lawn mower we kept at the back, and brought it out into the yard.

"What are ye doin' lad?" my grandfather asked.

Without looking at him, I said, "Dad wants this grass cut before it rains."

I stayed out in the yard, mowing it, trimming it, raking up the freshly cut grass blades…I stayed out there for a good two and a half hours. Even after the rain started falling, I continued to work. I moved like an automated robot, but my mind was in a whirl. Thoughts of my disrespect made for self-loathing. I didn't want to face my grandparents and my sister, knowing that I had prevented them from seeing my father one last time. And I thought of how Eva, who was to marry Clifford Deans in a little less than two months from now, would probably have my grandfather walk her down the aisle.

It was sometime later that I found out the man who had entered La Bella Luna had mowed down one young waiter, five women, and four men…one of which was my father. Numerous others were injured, as my mother and the young man I'd seen at the hospital had been. The shooter was a member of Detroit's notorious Purple Gang. He was Carlo Andolucci, and the next day, he had walked into the Detroit Police Department and confessed to the killings.

CHAPTER SEVEN

Helen answered her phone after I heard it ring in my ear three times. It was just before 8:00 a.m.

"Helen? This is Sam. I'm glad you're up for the day," I greeted her.

"Well, *of course* I'm up for the day! What do you think; I answer the phone in my sleep? Now, what do you want?"

I sighed loudly. She could be one mean old cuss. "I want to know if my grandmother is there."

She hesitated. She hesitated way too long.

"Helen?"

"What? What do you want?" she asked again, stalling for time, trying to think of a good answer.

I smiled. "Does my grandmother happen to be at your house?"

I could tell she lowered the mouthpiece of the phone, but didn't cover it…as if moving it directly away from one's lips would prevent the person on the other end from hearing anything at all.

"It's that grandson of yours and he wants to know if you're here," she said in a lowered tone to someone; that someone being my grandmother…I was now sure she was there.

"Tell him 'no,' I don't want to talk to him," I heard Gran say.

"No! And she doesn't want to talk to you! I think she went to Philadelphia!" she all but yelled.

In the background I could hear Gran's protests. "*Philadelphia*? Why on earth would I go to *Philadelphia*?"

Helen had moved the phone from her mouth again. "Well, don't you know someone in Philadelphia?" she asked.

"No, I don't *know* anyone in *Philadelphia*! I've never even *been* to that state before! Oh, you; give me that phone!" I heard Gran say. Once she held the receiver she snapped, "What do you want?"

Suddenly, I found it hard to continue, but I made myself say, "Gran, listen; I know you're upset with me and I don't blame you. Let me come over and bring you home."

"No!" she yelled. "I think I might stay here a month!"

In the background, Helen objected. "A *month*? You most certainly will *not*!"

"Come on, Gran. We can talk once we get back here," I pleaded.

"NO!" she shouted, and then there was a click on the line. She'd hung up on me.

Well, the important thing was that I now knew where my grandmother had gone. She was safe, and for the time being, that was all that mattered to me.

****

I spent the remainder of the morning mowing the lawn in the front and the back. I then uncoiled the garden hose and sprayed it, watching as the cold droplets of moisture were absorbed rapidly by the thirsty roots. With the high temperatures of late, I had to be careful not to let the grass burn and wither. By eleven o'clock it was already eighty-seven degrees in the sun. Sitting under the tree in a lawn chair in the backyard, I trained the cold flowing water onto my feet and arms. Thoughts of Gran getting sprayed in the face yesterday made me smile and I, too, turned the hose to flood my head.

Despite it being a holiday—Independence Day—the neighborhood was relatively quiet. There didn't seem to be any activity at Albie and Bobby's house, and I wondered if they had gone picnicking for the day. Gran and I had talked of maybe going to Belle Isle to sit under the shade of the trees and watch the boats out on the water, but I guess that was out of the question now. It was probably just as well. The small recreational island that sat out in the Detroit River between the city of Detroit and Canada was probably swarming with visitors and I didn't much feel like being in a crowd. As the day progressed, though, I didn't feel much like being alone, either. If the Double Shot had been opened, I would've headed over there to get a drink or two...or maybe more. But it was Sunday, besides being a holiday, and it certainly was not open for business.

I doused my whole head under the flow of cold water one more time and then rose to shut the faucet off. Once inside the house, I opened the icebox, seeing what there was to eat. I grabbed two large tomatoes and a handful of green onions. After washing them, I placed them on a plate and took it into the dining room along with the salt and pepper shakers. Turning on the radio, I found the station airing the Detroit Tiger baseball game. They were playing the New York Yankees here in Detroit at Briggs Stadium. The ballpark was originally known as Bennett Park, but at some point during my childhood, the stadium's name was changed to Navin Field, after the team's then owner, Frank Navin. When Navin died, Walter Briggs took over as owner of the team, expanding the field, and it had been renamed to honor him five years ago.

Today's game was going to be a doubleheader. I sat in the rocking chair and listened while I ate my salted tomatoes and onions. The voice of Harry "Slug" Heilmann, a former player for the Tigers, reached my ears and pulled me in with his blow by blow description of the game. The team had signed a rookie pitcher this season, and I was keeping my eye on him. He was Frank "Stubby" Overmire. The twenty-four year old from the Grand Rapids area would be used in relief. I'd read somewhere that Detroit was starting him off at a salary of thirty-six hundred dollars a year; not bad for a kid his age. I listened while the Detroit Tigers tucked their tails in the first game, losing to New York 1-0. The second was going much better for the home team.

After the first few innings, I went to the phone in the kitchen on the wall near the back door and dialed Helen's number again.

"May I speak to my grandmother?" I asked politely after Helen had answered.

She didn't say anything, but must've handed the instrument to Gran.

"Yes?"

"Gran, why don't you come home? I've got the game on and we can listen to it. You can have a cold beer. I'll come and get you," I said. She didn't respond. "Gran, I'm sorry about last night. I love you, you know."

"I love you, too, but I'm not coming home!"

For the second time, she hung up on me. I sighed and crossed to the icebox, getting out one of those cold beers and returned to listening to the game. Only this time, I listened from the living room. I eased back on the couch, putting my bare feet up on the coffee table, and uncapped the

Champagne Velvet beer. Taking a swig of the frosty beverage, I heard Slug Heilmann shriek with excitement when a Tiger batter batted in two runs. I listened through the whole game, only dozing once briefly. The Tigers clobbered the Yankees by a score of 6-0.

After the game, I turned the radio to a music station and meandered throughout the house, picking up the newspaper, cleaning out Shamus's litter box, and finally, cooking myself a huge plate of scrambled eggs and toast. By seven-thirty that evening, I felt myself growing tired. After all, I'd been up and awake since three-fifteen that morning. But I was feeling restless, unsettled. My mind wouldn't leave well enough alone and I truly wanted to talk to someone.

I went to the telephone on the kitchen wall and dialed the New York City exchange for Patti Ann. Patti Ann was a woman I'd met only a couple of months back when I was working on a case for my friend, Johnny Delbeck. He and his wife, Grace, had taken in her niece and she'd gone missing. When I learned that someone saw her walk into a boutique in Dearborn, the city in which Johnny and Grace lived, I'd followed up on the lead. The boutique was owned by a strikingly attractive woman...Patti Ann. The attraction was mutual, I figured, since she agreed to a date with me. What I didn't know was that a deal was in the works for her to rent space in New York City in which to open a second shop. I'd seen very little of her in these last couple of months, only getting together when she returned home for a few days at a time, but we always had fun and enjoyed each other's company. We didn't rank the status of "a couple"...yet. I was working on it and that was darn difficult because of the distance between us. The last time she'd been in Detroit was the second week in June, and that was only for two nights. I longed to talk to her now, to tell her of my father's death and of Sophia Andolucci's visit to my office.

The blonde beauty answered after three rings. She sounded out of breath, like she'd been just coming in from somewhere when she heard the phone ring.

"Hey, there," I said. "Did I catch you at a bad time?"

****

It was only going on half past eight on Sunday night, but I was bushed. I climbed on top of the sheets and laid in the dark, only in my underwear, thinking what a miserable day this had turned out to be. Gran was mad at me, and who knew how long she'd stay away. Calling Patti Ann had been a mistake. I was right in thinking I'd caught her at a bad time. She didn't sound like her usual self, and didn't seem excited to hear my voice. She'd been rushing to get ready to go out for the night, and I found that out when I'd heard the man's voice call out, "Will you be long, darling? We've got to make the theater for 8:00." And *that's* when she'd gotten all tongue-tied. She told me she would call me within the week, and we left it at that. Somehow, I doubted that call would ever come through. What I thought so important to tell her, she would never find out.

Well, it was bound to happen, with her living in New York and me in Detroit. I supposed we never really even had a shot at a relationship. Still, it stung, and I suddenly felt as though I'd just lost my best friend, even though I was just getting to know her. It was as though I'd just lost Dee Dee, my ex-wife, all over again. I felt empty and lonely. You would think that a man of my age could get along without his grandmother for a day or two, and I could...but I found myself missing her terribly.

CHAPTER EIGHT

On Monday morning, I woke with a new attitude. If Patti Ann had met someone else, that was fine by me. Who needed her? "Not I," said the face staring back at me from the bathroom mirror. And as far as Gran was concerned, I wasn't going to beg her to come home. I'd leave her alone for a day or two. If she could be stubborn, well, then I could, too.

After showering, I ate some toast while reading the comic book the kids from next door had given me. I read it, and then I re-read it. By ten in the morning, I'd pretty much decided on staying home and not going to the office. The day was totally wasted and non-productive, but pleasantly so. I was enjoying this rare solitude. The temperature was a bit cooler than it had been the last couple of weeks. It was in the low eighties today, and I sat outside watering the lawn again, while Shamus meowed out the window at me.

At two-thirty, I entered the house and turned on the wireless. Lying down on the couch I snoozed to the music of Glenn Miller, Stan Kenton, and Kay Kyser. As my eyes closed with sleepiness, I felt a wonderful breeze brush over my body from the open front parlor windows.

Fully awake by a quarter to five, I was hungry and feeling antsy. No longer did I enjoy being alone. I didn't know what to do with myself. There was nothing to clean and I wasn't going to read the comic book again. I rose from the couch and entered the kitchen, where Shamus was lapping up water from his bowl. Next to it sat another bowl, but it was empty. I fed the cat and then jumped in the shower. Tonight wasn't going to be spent alone doing nothing. I was going out for the evening.

****

The Double Shot was quiet at this hour. It was just going on half past six. The interior of the bar was dimmed and my eyes needed a few moments to adjust. I could make out a young couple sitting at a corner table, heads bent together talking and laughing quietly, a beer in front of each of them. Neamon, one of the owners, was standing behind the counter that stretched along the back wall, reading a newspaper, a cup of coffee to his left. He looked up when I entered.

"Hey, what is this? Twice in one week? I'm surprised to see you in so soon." He grabbed a damp rag and began wiping the surface in front of where I was heading to sit. "What'll ya have, Sam?"

"Give me a scotch on the rocks, and what's your specials?" I asked as I hopped up on one of the worn black leather upholstered stools.

"Got some really good corned beef and cabbage, and the toasted turkey sandwich ain't so bad, either. Of course, I can make ya anything ya want."

"Corned beef sounds good," I said.

Once he set my scotch in front of me, he turned to a set of burners behind the bar, stirring something in a large pot. Neamon took a plate from one of the shelves overhead and began to fill it with corned beef, carrots, cabbage, potatoes and onions. The aroma alone was making my mouth water. I took a hefty gulp of my drink and watched him while he worked. He wasn't a large man; he stood maybe five feet nine inches tall. His head was covered with a good amount of thick, wavy, silver hair, even though he had to be five or six years shy of the age of fifty. It had been that way ever since I'd met him. In the last few years, he'd packed on a good twenty or thirty pounds that had accumulated around his middle, making his belt hard to see. His face was ruddy and pock marked, his nose appearing as though it had been broken more than once during his lifetime. In his younger years, Neamon Riley had worked on the railroad, but because of some type of accident, he'd injured his back, making it impossible for him to continue performing the heavy manual labor he'd been accustomed to doing. Back in the later months of 1935, after recovering during a number of weeks, he'd talked his wife's cousin, Finney, into purchasing the bar with him. Actually, Finney was the real money man behind the business, hardly ever stepping foot in The Double Shot. Neamon ran the joint, with little help, day and night–and that made his wife, Lena, complain day and night. Still, you couldn't find a nicer couple to know. They'd give you the shirts off their backs if they felt you were in trouble or in need.

My eyes swept the room again. The black and white tiled flooring needed a good cleaning; the atmosphere smelled stale with thirty-five-cent cigar smoke, and the walls could have used a layer of fresh paint. It was a hole in the wall, really, but I felt comfortable here, and the drink prices were very reasonable.

Neamon placed the plate in front of me.

"You expect me to eat all that?" I asked, looking at the huge portion he'd set before me.

He shrugged. "Eat what ya want of it. Hey, Sam, ya want some horseradish? Lena made some good horseradish, but ya only need a little. It's powerful stuff," he said while reaching under the counter. "Here ya go."

I uncapped the jar and spooned a bit of it onto my plate. Just from the strong aroma that made its way to my nostrils, I knew I should be cautious. I dug in with gusto, suddenly realizing how very hungry I was. The meal was delicious, but within a matter of minutes, I felt full, not able to continue. I was stuffed and couldn't eat another bite, and shoved the plate to the side, feeling guilty for leaving half of it.

Catching Neamon looking at the uneaten portion, I said, "It was great, it's just too much."

The man shrugged and slid the plate over in front of himself and, using my fork, began to eat what I couldn't. Before he could polish it off, two young men came in and sat at the other end of the bar. Neamon excused himself to wait on them.

I pulled out a cigarette, lit it, and sipped at my scotch. Overhead fans whirred softly, pushing the smoky air around; not eliminating it, but spreading it to the four corners of the room. The same thoughts I'd had for a couple of days filled my mind now—thoughts of my father. I didn't want to dwell on what was long past, but it seemed I couldn't escape the memories that were making themselves one with my mind. If simple activities like listening to a baseball game, cleaning up around the house, or a change of scenery couldn't relieve me of my torment, I could always try making myself one with a bottle of scotch. Maybe that would help.

I tipped the glass and tasted the last drop on my tongue and then held it up in a signal to the bar owner that I needed a refill. He noticed and meandered over, poured me another without a word, and then returned to his interrupted conversation.

The juke box in the front corner of the room was sitting lonely and silent. I thought that the jazzy sound of Cab Calloway might mask the dreariness which had permeated my mind. Reaching into my pocket, I pulled out six steel pennies and a nickel. It was all the change I had. I shoved the coins back in and took a gulp of my drink. After putting my cigarette out in the clear glass ashtray that was in front of me, I immediately lit another one. When I looked straight across from me, into the filmy mirror that hung on the wall between the shelves of plates, condiments and bottles of liquor, I thought I saw Connor Flanagan staring back at me. It was funny how I'd never noticed that I was becoming more and more the image of my father.

I was torn away from my own reflection by movement to my left. It was the couple I'd seen with their heads together at the back table, ready to settle their bill. Looking at them, I noticed the gal was a bit on the pudgy side and rather plain in appearance. I glanced at the fellow she was with and knew why he'd chosen her as his date. He wasn't any more attractive than she was. Neamon rang them out and wished them a good night at the cash register. As he was going past me, I held out my glass for another refill. His eyes lowered to what was in my hand, and then rose up to meet my gaze. He grabbed it from me and turned around to fill it once again. When he turned back, there was a clear liquid with a few cubes of ice floating on top in the glass. He set it in front of me; and started heading toward the men he'd been conversing with.

"Hey," I stopped him. "What's this?" I said with an edge in my tone, gesturing toward the drink.

"It's water," he answered.

"Water? What's with the water? I didn't ask for water!" I gave him a hard stare. "My money isn't good here?"

He slowly returned to me and said, almost under his breath, "Listen, you've only been here going on a half hour. Why don't you slow it down a bit?"

"Yeah? And what's it to *you*?"

My face was locked in a stern expression; my lips taught. Neamon, on the other hand, knit his brows and squinted with his eyes. His look told me he was confused by my behavior. I didn't say another word.

Finally Neamon asked, "Hey, what's going on? I've never seen you like this before. What's eatin' at you tonight?"

"Nothing!" I said it with stiffness in my voice.

He leaned on the surface of the bar in front of me and laced his fingers together. "How long I known you, Sam? How long you known me? Seven, maybe eight years? Now, I'm a bartender and that's sorta like bein' one of them shrinks. You're the customer and you come in here and tell me what's buggin' you and I listen. Now I never seen you act this way, so I say somethin' is eatin' at ya."

I stared at him for five seconds more and then my resolve melted like a bowl of ice cream in hundred degree heat. I ran the palm of my hand over my face and sighed.

"Aw, damn it, forget I said anything. I didn't mean it. Just a bad day, I guess. Sorry about that."

"No, now, come on. Things don't bother you like this. Now what's got you wantin' to blur the world in a bottle of scotch?"

I looked at him as he picked his front teeth with a fingernail, and then I told him everything.

CHAPTER NINE

When I was done with my story of what happened back in April of 1924, and told him how Mrs. Sophia Andolucci, widow of Mr. Carlo Andolucci, had dredged it all up for me again, he whistled softly.

"No kiddin'! I knew your daddy was gone from this earth, but you never said how he left it."

"Yeah, well, that's the story."

"Of course, I remember when that happened," he said, "but it never made any sense to me." He was staring over my left shoulder, focusing on nothing, lost in thought.

"How's that?"

"Well, I remember being surprised. I couldn't believe a fella like Carlo Andolucci had done something like that."

"Why?" I asked; tautly.

Hearing the defiance in my voice, his eyes returned to my face. My expression dared him to go on…at his own risk.

"Well, do you remember soon after Lena and I were married?" He looked at me and waved his hand in the air. "Oh hell, 'course you don't! I didn't even know you back then. When we got married in '21, I was workin' at the bowlin' alley over on Fort Street settin' pins. It wasn't much of a job and it didn't pay much. I'd been lookin' for somethin' better, but only half-hearted. So, one day when I come in from work, I find Lena cryin' on the sofa. Seems she'd spent the day at her mother's and…well you know…they were discussin' women issues, I guess. Lena hadn't been feelin' all too well for a time there and her ma tells Lena that she must be in a family way. As for her cryin', well, I think that was just plain fear. After all, she was only nineteen when Neamon Jr. was born…still a young girl. Hell, I was a bit nervous, myself. Anyway, on my way home from work the next day, I stopped into Hibbard's Florist over there on Woodward."

He paused in his story to ask me if I remembered Emil Hibbard and his flower shop and I nodded that I did.

"Well, I sure didn't have much money on me, but I had enough for a carnation. I thought it might cheer her up—let her know that I loved her, you know? Anyway, we get to talkin'—Hibbard and me—and the next thing I know, he's offerin' me a side job. In addition to my job at the bowlin' alley, he wants me to show up three nights a week and do various things for him."

"At *night*?" I asked, surprised.

"Yeah," he said, waving his hand in the air. "Things like takin' walks around the shop, just to make sure everything was all right."

He stopped talking and just stared at me, as if waiting for me to understand what he was trying to tell me.

Finally, I had to ask him. "To see if everything was all right? What do you mean?" I took a sip of the water in front of me and then lit a cigarette.

"Well, seems nice old Emil Hibbard wasn't as squeaky clean as he appeared. Remember how he used to give the kids candy out in front of the flower shop in the summertime, Sam?"

"Yeah," I said after exhaling a lungful of smoke. I wondered what he was trying to get at and I could feel myself getting antsy...getting impatient.

"Down in the basement of the flower shop, he was runnin' a speakeasy." He straightened and crossed his arms over his chest, almost as though he were proud of the fact that he knew this and I had no idea whatsoever that the sweet Mr. Emil Hibbard was a criminal of sorts.

I had to blink twice. "Mr. *Hibbard*?"

"Yep," he nodded, with emphasis.

I still didn't see how this story of Neamon's was going to tie together with Carlo Andolucci.

"Okay, so what's the rest of it? How does Andolucci fit in with Hibbard?"

"Well, that's just it," he began.

Neamon Riley told me that in addition to being a sort of lookout for Emil Hibbard, he was also a general errand boy for the man; running for sandwiches, cleaning his office and private bathroom on the lower level, and hauling the stock of liquor down the stairs to the drinking and gaming area. While he'd only done it for a year, he'd brought in some badly needed money from his employment with the kindly old florist. And during his one year of employment, he'd learned a bit more about the man who employed him. He'd learned that Emil Hibbard didn't like to part with his money once he earned it. He'd learned that Emil Hibbard wasn't so fond of handing over the "protection" money that Abe Saperstein and his brothers—commonly referred to as The Purple Gang, Detroit's notorious group of thugs—demanded for their services. And he told me of an incident that had occurred a few days after Christmas of 1923. Old man Hibbard was in his office, sitting at his desk, and Neamon had just finished up sanitizing the guy's personal bathroom. As he turned out the light and put his hand on the knob of the door to open it farther so he could exit, he heard the outer door to the office open and someone enter. Neamon saw his boss take on a look of apprehension and stand, facing his newly arrived visitor. Sensing something, Neamon ducked out of sight behind the door and stood in the darkened room, barely breathing, eying the situation through the crack. He saw a good looking young man with jet black hair slicked back away from his face, wearing an expensive tweed overcoat. The visitor was of medium height and average build from what he could tell. As the man stood, facing his employer, a strong scent of expensive and manly cologne wafted to Neamon's nostrils. He removed fine black leather gloves as he greeted Mr. Hibbard.

"Good evening, my friend."

"What do you want, Andolucci?" Hibbard's voice cracked with nervousness.

The younger man raised his hands, palms up and asked in his slight foreign accent, "Ah, now is that any way to greet a friend? And I think you know why I'm here. Mr. Saperstein seems to be missing a payment from you. You're late to the tune of five days. I've just come to rectify this situation for him, capiche?"

"I don't have it right now. Tell Saperstein to give me a few more days," Emil responded timidly.

"That isn't so good, my friend. He's already waited for what's due him. And don't you think Mr. Saperstein has earned this small fee since he keeps you safe from those who would like to destroy your little lucrative business?"

Neamon witnessed Andolucci slide his hands inside his overcoat pockets and saw his boss flinch with fright as a cold sweat rolled down the sides of his own face and neck.

"Easy, easy," Carlo Andolucci said; with a smile on his lips. "There's nothing to fear."

He pulled his hands back out and displayed them to the older man. They were empty, holding nothing. He then pointed to Mr. Hibbard's left hand. The first two fingers on the florist's hand were bent at a painful angle.

"What happened there?"

"You know damn well what happened! One of 'the boys' did this number on me!"

Andolucci shook his head. "That's a shame. You see what can happen when you disappoint Mr. Saperstein? Come on, he's a good guy. You just need to be fair here. I'll tell you what. I'll give you those few days and smooth it over with him…but here's what I want you to do, and it will be our little secret, capiche?"

The bar owner told me that he'd been a witness to Carlo Andolucci telling Hibbard that he wanted the old man to bandage up his left arm in a sling and wear it that way for at least a month, maybe a week or two more. Abe Saperstein would be told that Mr. Hibbard was left with a definite message. He strongly cautioned the florist not to deviate from what he was telling him to do, and also warned him not to let on to anyone that the sling wasn't really needed. The young collector would be back in three days time to collect the money owed…and he stressed that at that time, he didn't want to make the man's hands a matching set.

I stared at Neamon when he was done telling the story. I just shrugged and said, "Okay…so?"

The bar owner softly slapped the top of the counter in front of me. "Well, gee, Sam! Don't you see? The guy goes out of his way to avoid roughin' up the old man! Even to the point of puttin' himself in danger if Saperstein ever found out! I mean, hell, out on the streets, Andolucci was known as

Carlo 'the Confessor' Andolucci. Eh, the guy toted a set of rosary beads around with him, and every time he had to 'send a message,' he'd pull them out and ask for forgiveness. At least that's what others said. I guess the guy was a strict Catholic from what's been told. And I never heard one darn story that this young fella whacked someone. Maybe caused some pain, but no whackin'. So I figure—and don't go gettin' the hair up on the back of your neck when I say this—that this guy ain't like the rest of 'em. I kinda looked at it like he was the 'good' bad guy. Know what I mean? He's got a heart in an odd sorta way. He doesn't really want to *hurt* anyone. So, I remember when that shootin' happened in that fancy restaurant and I remember thinkin', Andolucci did *that*? This guy doesn't want to bust a knuckle…feels guilty when he does, but he goes into a full restaurant and kills a bunch of innocents, along with the guy that's intended to get the lead? It didn't make sense to me. Anyway, I could see the writin' on the wall. I quit workin' for Hibbard right after the New Year. I didn't want to end up as one of the schmucks in the line of fire when the blastin' started. Hell, I had a kid who wasn't but a few months old and a wife to take care of. And it wasn't long after that I found the job at the railroad. Funny thing though; old man Hibbard died of a heart attack when he was eighty-four, the lucky cuss."

The door to The Double Shot opened and Neamon looked up and beyond me. I said nothing as I rubbed my chin, pondering the story he'd just told me.

"Hey," he called out. "Your usual?"

The new customer must have nodded, because I didn't hear a reply and Neamon grabbed a martini glass from the shelf. He lifted a bottle of premium gin and began to pour. Before serving it to whoever had come in, the bar owner turned to me, leaned closer, and said in a low tone, "Now *this* is the guy you should be talkin' to."

CHAPTER TEN

I introduced myself to Mr. Herschel Sussermann and he cordially asked me to sit opposite him in the booth. The first thing I noticed about him was the glasses he wore. The lenses were tinted a dark green, appearing almost black, and I couldn't see the eyes behind them. The second thing I was struck by was his nose. It wasn't a wide nose, but it was long and curved downward, with two prominent bumps in its descent. His hair was full, wavy, and a pearly white, with streaks of dull yellow running through it. He wore a dark gray suit that was fraying slightly at his wrists, along with a white shirt, and a red bow tie at the base of his neck. I told him what I was interested in speaking to him about.

"What are you drinking, my friend? May I buy you one?"

I looked down at the glass of water that I had carried with me from the bar. "No thank you. This water will do."

"Water? Hmm," he muttered. "You'll have to forgive my spectacles. The lighting hurts my eyes of late."

I frowned. Lighting in The Double Shot was clearly muted. Righting my expression almost immediately, I didn't want the old gentleman to observe my confusion. I would have guessed him to be in his late sixties, and it was confirmed for me that he was having trouble with his vision when he gingerly slid his hand along the table top until his fingers touched the stem of his martini glass. He lifted it to his lips and took a sip, making an exclamation of satisfaction after swallowing. Turning his head slightly to his right, he called out, "Did you add olives?"

"Yes sir," Neamon called back. "Two of 'em, but I'm all out of toothpicks. They're in the bottom of the drink."

"Ah, very good, my friend," Mr. Sussermann responded, and then he turned to me and asked, "May I inquire why you're here?"

I frowned again and repeated, "I'd like to ask you about your association with one Abe Saperstein."

"Well, that is old news. I haven't seen Abe in some time. I worked for him as his bookkeeper, but that was some years ago. I kept his books and he paid me well for it, but that's all I did in his organization. And, if truth be known, I never cared for the man. I didn't really care for *any* of the Saperstein brothers. He's not around here anymore. He's gone to the east coast."

"Well, let me tell you why I'm asking, sir."

Beginning with telling him that I was a private detective, I told him about Sophia Andolucci's visit to my office and what she had come to see me about.

"Carlo Andolucci," he said, pondering the name. "It does sound familiar; let me think. Like I said, I only kept his books and didn't want to know anything else. Abe had few working for him that weren't Jewish, though. Seems I ought to remember."

"That's okay, take your time," I said, trying to nudge his memory gently.

He took another sip of his gin and then rubbed his forehead while his eyes were slightly aimed at the table top. I noticed a twitching in his left cheek directly below the lower rim of his glasses and wondered if he was getting too stressed.

"It doesn't matter," I said, trying to put the man at ease. "I just wondered if you remembered him well enough to tell me what you thought of him."

"Well, if he worked for Abe in that capacity, he was nothing but scum. They all were," he said emphatically. "Who is this man supposed to have murdered, anyway?"

"A restaurant full of innocent people," I said. "My mother and father were eating at La Bella Luna that night. My father never came home again."

Herschel Sussermann sighed with regret, and then tilted his head up and said, "La Bella Luna?"

I nodded, but then realized he probably hadn't seen me do so.

"Yes," I said.

"I remember that! This Carlo Andolucci...was he the one who confessed to it at the police station the day after?"

My heartbeat quickened with excitement and anticipation of what he was remembering. I didn't have a chance to answer in the affirmative, because he went on speaking.

"Carlo Andolucci, I *do* think I remember him! Hadn't been in the country long, as I recall. Came from somewhere like Italy or Sicily...could've been Malta."

"Yes," I said; eagerly.

"If it's the man I'm thinking of, he was young and one day I remember he came in and I just out and out asked him why in the world he was working for Abe Saperstein. My memory isn't what it used to be, but I must have asked him that for a reason. I believe I felt that he didn't belong with Abe's organization, but I can't recall why. I remember him looking at me and telling me a man had to do what a man had to do to take care of his family. Yes, now I remember.

This Andolucci fellow smiled wide and then said to me, 'Mr. Herschel,'—he always called me Mr. Herschel—'my wife informs me we are expecting an addition to the family.' If it's the same young man I am picturing, he was always dressed nicely, wearing very good clothes. Always looked handsome and well-kept, if you know what I mean. Yes, he didn't belong with that bunch of no good sons of bitches."

Mr. Sussermann shook his head and reached out for his martini. I was trying to assess what I was learning about the man who had taken my father's life and it wasn't jiving with what I had always thought I knew. But how could I trust that who Mr. Herschel Sussermann was describing was, in fact, Carlo Andolucci? He seemed to struggle with his memory. Yet, the man he was talking about *did* sound like the one Neamon had described physically to me.

Suddenly, the old man spoke, asking me, "Did you say La Bella Luna?"

"Yes."

"That's where that shooting was all those years ago. Abe ordered that," he said. "Seems he wanted a man taken care of who had been stealing some of the liquor that he delivered to the Purples. I suppose the gentleman was taking a little from each bottle of the supply every delivery and hid the fact by making up the difference with water." He shook his head. "That was real sad. The guy wasn't a bad man. He had a wife and around a dozen kids to raise...a real shame. I would assume he was selling what he took on the side for his own gain. And what real difference would it have made to Abe? He was raking in plenty of dough from all over the place, the lousy, cold-hearted fat-head. I could hear him screaming about it in his office a couple of doors down. He was ordering this hit. I think that one you're asking about was in there with that other little bastard. We could hear him yelling through two walls, and when I looked up, the kid was all wide-eyed and had an uncomfortable look on his face. I remember Abe telling where the mark would be the next night, and I believe he said he'd be at La Bella Luna."

Hearing how he felt about Saperstein and the men who worked for him, I wondered why this gentleman, too, chose to work there. With training as a bookkeeper, couldn't he have gotten a position elsewhere? It seemed he would have had little trouble in securing other employment.

"Who was the other guy in the office with Saperstein and Andolucci?" I inquired.

"That rotten bastard…let me think. Bobby, Billy…whatever. His last name was Levinthal. I felt shame he carried a Jewish name. He'd put an ice pick through your eye just for looking at him twice, and smile while he was doing it. He actually enjoyed that sort of thing. Hey, you might want to talk to Nardini; Mario Nardini. I think he's still in town. Outside of the brothers, he was Abe's right-hand man, handling some part of the business. I don't know what part now; my memory, you know? And then there's always that gal who sang."

"What gal who sang?" I was mentally making notes of these names. Levinthal, Nardini…and now, who?

"That girlfriend of Abe's. Of course, Abe was married and had a family, but he kept this woman in jewels and furs. Aw, damn it, what was her name? Kathleen something. Kathleen Paulson, something like that. Pretty little thing. She sang in one of his clubs."

He tipped his glass, draining the contents of it, and yelled out for another. After Neamon delivered it and went back to the bar, I asked about the woman.

"You think Kathleen Paulson is still in town?"

"Who?"

"Saperstein's girlfriend; the one he was keeping."

"I don't know any Kathleen Paulson. Abe's gal was Kate Nelson. Pretty little thing," he said.

"But you say this Mario Nardini still has a place in the city?" I was trying to get the people straight in all of this and make sure he didn't change his story on this guy.

"Mario Nardini? Nah, Kate wasn't *his* gal; she was Abe's. Nardini was high up in the organization, though…one of Abe's right-hand men."

He startled me by doing a complete one-eighty on me by mentioning another name.

"Did you say you knew Eliana?"

"Eliana? Now who is she?"

"Who is *she*? She was my wife! The best thing that's ever happened to me. I thought you said you knew her. She's gone now," he said with deep sadness in his voice. "Know what her name means in Hebrew? It means 'my Lord has answered,' and that's exactly what He did. He answered my prayer the day I met her."

"It's eight-fifteen," Neamon called from the bar.

Herschel Sussermann finished off his second martini in three big swallows, set the glass on the table, and started to slide out of the booth. He rose to his feet, reached into the booth behind him, and lifted a cane off the seat. He turned back to me.

"Got to go now. Maybe I'll see you again sometime, young man. I'll tell you about Eliana. She was Abe Saperstein's sister, you know." He tipped the gray fedora that he'd just placed on his head and cautiously walked toward the door. I suddenly knew why he stayed with The Purples, doing their books—Abe Saperstein was his brother-in-law.

****

It was going on nine-thirty and I was just about finished with the second scotch on the rocks that I'd ordered since the departure of the older Jewish gentleman. Neamon had been busy serving other customers. The place had gradually filled up, but now he came over to stand in front of me.

"So, interestin' fella Herschel Sussermann is, huh?" he asked as he leaned on the bar.

"Yeah, if you can decipher what he's trying to say," I said, rolling my eyes.

"Hey!" Neamon said, as he straightened. "Don't go talkin' like that!"

"Well, what's wrong with him?"

"He's only got a thing growin' in his head is all. You'd have a bit of trouble, too, if that was happenin' to you. Doc gave him three weeks and that was four months ago. But I can tell he's gettin' a bit worse. Some things fade in his mind at times, and other times, he seems all right. He comes in five nights a week at exactly seven-thirty, orders precisely two gin martinis, and leaves at exactly eight-fifteen to get home for his radio programs."

I sheepishly apologized, then pulled out the money to pay my tab. I handed Neamon some extra cash to cover the two martinis that Sussermann drank. The old guy left in a hurry and didn't bother settling with the bar owner. He slid the additional money back across the surface to me.

"No need, Sam. He comes in the first of every month and hands me a twenty and a five to pay for all the drinks he'll order throughout the weeks. Does that each and every month since he's gotten that bad news from the doc, and he nowhere near drinks twenty-five dollars worth. Says he doesn't want to leave me hangin' if he's not here one day." Neamon shook his head while looking toward the door to his saloon. "Gee, I'm gonna miss that old gent. He's as good as gold."

CHAPTER ELEVEN

By nine o'clock on Tuesday morning, I'd showered, shaved, and had breakfast. Even my bed was made. I was sitting at the kitchen table enjoying a second cup of coffee, observing Shamus as he kept watch from the window sill. Thoughts of my evening at The Double Shot occupied the whole of me. I'd wanted to get pie-eyed last night, but this morning I was extremely grateful I had not…even if it *did* take Neamon to guide me in that direction. For some strange reason, I was experiencing a mild sensation of calmness, and I was enjoying this suspension of inner turmoil. What I'd learned while at Neamon's was definitely interesting, to say the least; but it didn't serve to veer me onto the path of taking this case for Mrs. Sophia Andolucci. No, I wasn't the man to do the job. She could travel on to the next investigator in her search for justice.

Shamus jumped down from the sill and trotted out of the kitchen, through the dining room, and into the front parlor. He turned to the left, out of my line of sight. Scooting my chair back, I knew I had to fill his dish with the little tuna we had left in the icebox before I headed out to work for the day. I needed to bring some money in, and I couldn't do it by staying away from the office. Having done that, I turned on the faucet, allowing it to flow until it reached its coldest temperature. I was filling his water bowl when I heard the front screen door open. For a split second I envisioned that the cat had somehow gotten the darn thing unlatched, but immediately chuckled inside at the image. But who could it be? My head turned to the left, my eyes bypassing the dining room and settling on the room beyond it. Gran came into my field of view.

"Hey!" I said, jovially. I was darned glad to see her. I placed the full bowl of cold, fresh water next to the dish of tuna and went to greet my grandmother. She had come in and immediately slumped down onto the sofa. When I entered the room, she had her hand resting on her chest and her breathing was labored.

"Are you okay?" I asked, feeling a bit of alarm.

She nodded and laid her head against the back of the cushion, closing her eyes.

"What's wrong?" I persisted.

She shook her head, still struggling with getting enough air into her lungs. She finally rose to an upright position and asked if I could bring her a glass of water, and I didn't hesitate in getting it. Sitting next to her, I rubbed her back gently as she drank.

"Ah, there," she said when done. "I'm feeling a bit better now." And then suddenly, she all but yelled, "That dern Helen!"

I jumped at her outburst. "What on earth…? What happened?"

"I'm not talking to you!" she replied.

I rose from the sofa and headed toward my bedroom.

"Where are you going?" she asked when I emerged with my fedora in hand.

"Well, I'll make not talking to me easy for you. I'm going into the office and won't be home until late. Don't hold dinner."

I had no real plans for myself after I would be closing the Woodward Avenue office, but I sure wasn't going to spend time walking on egg shells around my grandmother. No, I'd just stay away as long as I could for today. She stared at me for a few seconds and then buried her face in her hands, emitting long wails. It was the most pitiful attempt at crying I'd ever heard.

"Oh, come on! You can do better than that, can't you?"

Gran parted her middle fingers, exposing dry eyes, and looked up at me.

"Well, don't ya even want to know why I'm mad at Helen?" she asked after lowering her hands to her lap.

"Gran," I said in a controlled tone. "I *asked* you that, but you said you weren't speaking to me."

"I'll just tell you this one thing, and then I won't speak to you."

I sighed, backed up to sit on the chair, and twirled my hat in my hands. Looking at her, I said, "Okay, shoot. Tell me what happened."

"She wants a maid, not a friend!" she screamed in a high-pitched voice. "She's been making me cook and clean ever since I got there, pretending she doesn't feel well! Well, she's got another think comin', because I'm not doing it anymore! I walked out before she even woke up this morning."

"You *what*? Are you telling me you *walked* home from Helen's?"

She put her hand to her chest and nodded her head.

"Yes, and if I would've keeled over on the way home, it would've served her right!"

"My God, woman; why didn't you call for me to pick you up? Gran, you've done some foolish things, but this takes the cake. You're lucky you made it home."

"I didn't want to use her phone. She probably would've made me pay for the call! And besides, I'm mad at you and I won't be speaking to you."

"Listen to me, Gran," I began, lowering my eyes to the fedora I still held in my hands. "I honestly didn't want to bring this up. I didn't want to upset you with this. But I can see I've upset you anyway with my stupid behavior. I'm terribly sorry for pushing you away like I did the other night, but I had something happen at the office on Saturday afternoon that I just didn't know how to handle."

I raised my eyes to hers and saw that she was waiting…waiting for me to go on and explain everything. I let out a long sigh and then told her all of it, right from the beginning. Once I started, it seemed as though I couldn't stop. It was as if a dam holding back my emotions for almost twenty years had burst. I found myself revealing all the guilt that I had tried to keep buried, and kept myself from barely thinking of, up until Sophia Andolucci had entered my office three days ago.

"And it was because of me that Grandpa felt so much stress in his last months, and that led to *his* death, too. I let everyone down by not coming home right away as I was told. We all lost precious time, Gran. Don't you see? Maybe if we had made it to the hospital on time—"

"You mean to tell me you've been carrying that around with you all these years?"

I didn't answer her, but surely the look on my face said it all. Exactly two weeks after my grandfather had walked Eva down the aisle, giving her to Clifford Deans in marriage, he had come into the parlor after eating dinner, lay down on the sofa, and told his wife he was mighty tired. He closed his eyes and, in that moment, took his last breath. A stroke had claimed him. He was gone as quick as that; no lingering, no suffering...but he was gone, nevertheless.

My grandmother remained silent. She sat on the sofa, examining her hands, which lay in her lap. She rubbed at her slightly knotted fingers and said nothing.

"What are you thinking, Gran?"

"Just how stupid you are." She said it very softly and with little emotion.

I recoiled from the sting of the remark, but didn't react—I had to *keep* myself from reacting.

After five seconds, she went on. "When I look back on it, I *have* had my share of sad times. When I lost the twins, I thought I was gonna die. You talk about stress? I didn't think I could go on, and if it weren't for your grandfather, I wouldn't have. I wish you could've seen them, Sam. They were the prettiest little girls you'd ever want to lay eyes on. Amelia and Abigail. Oh, your grandfather was so happy when I had those babies; but it's funny, you know? I had bad days; well, mostly bad days, but then there were days when I felt the Lord was right by my side. And, of course, I knew those little ones were with Him, and that seemed to comfort me for some hours; but it was in those hours that Paddy would break down and I'd have to be there to hold him up. Well, we seemed to get through that, and along came Roan. He looked most like your granddad, but he was quieter, gentler than Connor. And Paddy used to lie in bed beside me at night and say, 'Ruby, why doesn't that one fight back while the other is so filled with piss and vinegar?' I would just laugh and tell him I didn't know. But Paddy loved 'em both equally, even though Connor gave us a run for our money. He was the one that was sassy and always fightin' your grandfather on things," she said, and sighed. She raised her face and stared into the room before continuing. "And then that accident, with Roan falling from that building," she shuddered. "I was never more afraid of losing Paddy as I was then. He cried and he cried, just like he held an endless amount of tears and they were never gonna stop." Her eyes looked into mine and she said, "You didn't know your grandfather ever cried, did you?"

I shook my head, but inside I was thinking he must've cried. Everyone cried at some point.

"Well, I can tell you, Paddy would have liked to crawl in that box with your uncle right then and there…but we made it somehow. We had each other, just like we'd always had. And then your father…well, we'd lost them all. None of our children were left, and yet, we were still standing. Thank the good Lord for your mother. Paddy and I always felt Maeve was our very own daughter. When your grandfather went, she held me up when I just wanted to collapse and die myself."

She paused briefly, but when she started up again, she'd changed subjects. "You know what, dear? The older I get, the more I keep thinking of something when I was a little girl. I keep remembering how Papa used to take us for rides on hot summer nights. There were the four of us girls. Opal was the oldest, then Pearl, and then me, and then Garnetta was two years younger than me." She suddenly started giggling like a school girl. "Papa used to call us his little gems. Anyway, on a hot night, he'd hitch the horses up to the buggy and call out to us 'Who wants to go search for Injuns'?" She giggled again. "I was probably six or seven years old, and we'd climb in the back of the buggy, with Papa and Mother up front, and take a long ride through the trees and open fields. Of course, there weren't any Indians in this area then; they were farther out, but we girls didn't know it at the time. It was just Papa's way of relaxing us during the hot spells so we could sleep. I can still feel the wind whipping through my hair and the breeze on my face. We'd be in our pajamas, so when we got home again, we could climb right into bed. I'd give anything to go on one of those rides again," she sighed.

She startled me when she slapped the tops of her thighs. "You're stupid, Sam! Thinking all these years that you caused your grandfather's death, or at least thinking you helped it along. Who do you think you are, God? Do you really think that you have that kind of control over those things? Or that anybody does? I would suggest you spend more time in the Bible than you do; learn who's who, and see your place in this world. And as far as you thinking you stopped us from seeing Connor one last time; well, maybe that's our fault."

"What do you mean, your fault?"

"If you haven't known for all these years, I guess it's 'cause we never told you. Although, I don't know why we wouldn't have," she pondered. "Your father was never at that hospital. The doctor told us he'd died at the restaurant. I guess he was pretty much killed instantly. Yes, you should've come home when you were told, but that didn't change the situation."

Died at the restaurant? Died at the restaurant? I looked at Gran, but said nothing. She was right; this had never been told to me. I'd hung on to a belief all these years that just wasn't true. Suddenly, I had to find a way to let go of the imagined guilt I had carried around with me for half of my life. I had to let go of the shame and inner turmoil I carried around with me constantly. It would take some time.

She slapped the tops of her thighs again and asked, "All right, so what if it's all true?"

"What, Gran…what if what's all true?" I was bewildered. Where was she going now?

"Well, this Missus…whatever her name is. What if this Carlo fellow really was with his wife that night? What if someone else killed your father?"

I shook my head and started to protest. "Oh Gran, you can't think…."

"And why not?" she asked with a challenge in her voice.

Allowing myself to consider the possibility that Gran could be correct, I said, "It *has* struck me as odd that she would want this reopened. I mean, what would be the use? It doesn't make sense. Listen, I will look into this for a day or two, but if I don't find anything, I'm not taking this on. I'm not going to try to prove this guy didn't kill Dad, when I know he must've been involved in some way."

She rose from the sofa and smoothed her house dress. My grandmother started to walk toward the kitchen, with Shamus appearing from out of nowhere to follow her.

"Just look into it," she said as she disappeared from sight. "I want to know who was responsible for this before I die. He was my son."

Looking down at the hat I still held in my hands, her display of phony tears entered my mind. My grandmother—Ruby Flanagan—often displayed battiness in her reasoning. How much of *that* was a put on? Because, from what I'd just observed, the woman was one wise old bird.

CHAPTER TWELVE

Heading toward my office door, I could hear the clicking of keys on a typewriter bouncing off the walls in the hallway. Irwin's door, directly across from my office, was wide open. I poked my head in and saw Frankie Kirkendahl sitting behind the desk. Her reddish-brown hair was pulled back and up high in a ponytail today, and she wore a crisp pink summer blouse. I smiled when she looked up at me.

"Good morning, Frankie," I said sweetly.

"Well, it *was*," she replied with a scowl on her face.

I gave her my best injured expression. "Aw, now come on. Don't be rude. You're hurting my feelings."

I flinched, but laughed, when she picked up the long, pencil-like typewriter eraser and threw it at me, missing my face and hitting the door jamb.

"Can I interest you in getting a bite to eat with me at lunch time?" I persisted.

"Mr. Flanagan, don't you have work to do? *I* certainly do and you're preventing me from doing it! Now please leave."

Laughing, I crossed the hall to my door and unlocked it. The first thing I did was to raise the windows, allowing intermittent puffs of air to enter the space. The sun was shining brightly on my desk, but the temperature didn't appear as if it would reach eighty-five degrees today, and that was a good thing. The second thing I did was to lift the receiver off the base of the telephone and dial the precinct where I used to work at the Detroit Police Department. I asked to speak with Homicide Detective Bill McPherson, my old partner. He'd been on the force since 1923, the year before my father was killed. When we were partners during my four year stay, we walked the beat together and got on extremely well. Five years ago, he'd been promoted to the homicide division.

"Hey, Mac," I said when I heard his voice. "How are things going?"

"Sam? Let's just say things are going. I'm busy down here trying to get a perp to sing. The bank down on the corner of Gratiot was robbed last night, and a night watchman was shot up pretty bad. It's touch and go with him."

"Michigan National?" I inquired.

"Yep," he said.

"I won't keep you then. But listen, can you call me back sometime today? I need to ask you about something."

"Will do, buddy. Where will you be? Are you at home or the office?"

"The office."

After disconnecting, I grabbed a piece of paper and a pencil that had been sitting off to the side on my desk. I wrote out the names Levinthal, Kate Nelson and Mario Nardini. I didn't want to leave these to chance in my memory. If I was going to look into this at all, I needed to start at the beginning; though. I figured the day that Andolucci entered the police station to confess was the beginning. What I needed to know was who took that confession, and what the Purple Gang member said while confessing. Another thing I wanted to find out was who the attorney was that defended him. I was hoping that Mac could give me the answers.

Movement out in the hall made me look up from my desk. A tall man in white coveralls stood just outside Irwin's door. He was carrying brushes and a can of paint. I saw Irwin come into view and meet him at the door. The little guy handed the painter a piece of paper and the man got busy. Irwin must've hired this gent to paint lettering on the outside of the upper frosted glass portion of the doorway to his office. My own sign had been painted six years ago when I opened up the agency. I rose from my desk and bypassed the man, leaving my door standing open. Until Mac's call came in, I wasn't going to leave, but I was growing a bit hungry.

Taking the stairs down to the street level, I thought I'd check out Hooch's stand for a piece or two of fruit. I was in luck and bought a peach and an apple. He had no bananas today. When I returned, the painter had already begun his work. I watched him while I ate and marveled at what a steady hand he had. He was using gold paint to adorn the glass. My lettering was done in black. He held my attention for a good twenty minutes before my telephone rang. I grabbed it on the first ring, not wanting the noise to startle him. It didn't seem to as he perfectly filled in an L.

"Flanagan Investigations," I said into the mouthpiece.

"It's Mac, Sam."

"Oh, Mac thanks for getting back to me. I'd like to ask you about something. Do you remember back in '24 when Carlo Andolucci came in and confessed to the shooting at La Bella Luna?"

"Barely, why? That's where your parents were, right?" he asked.

"Yeah, but I want to know who he talked to when he came in that day. I want to know what he said. And did he have a lawyer? If so, I want to find out who defended him."

"Gee, that's a long time ago and I was still pretty new here, but I can ask around and call you back," he offered.

"Do that, will you, Mac?"

We ended our call and I returned to watching the man do his job across the hall. About two thirds down on the glass, he was painting "Attorney at Law" in a straight line, and it was looking mighty good.

I only had to wait fifteen minutes before Mac's return call came in.

"Yeah, I got some information for you. A detective at the time named Ralph Wozniak took Andolucci's statement, but he's long since been retired. Moved to Florida years ago and no one has kept in touch, so I don't have an address or contact number for you. But the chief says that Andolucci came in the next day around three in the afternoon, looking all decked out in his fine duds, and very politely asked to speak to someone. He told the desk sergeant he wanted to tell someone about a crime he'd committed. The chief says it didn't go to trial, but he was assigned an attorney from the public defender's office. Seems Andolucci didn't want to hire his own lawyer. I guess the guy who was assigned to the case was named Wright. Chief told me it was Ulysses Wright."

"The guy's name was Wright?" I asked, astounded.

"Yeah, why? You know him?"

"No, but I may know his son. It would be one hell of a coincidence, though."

"And Sam, the chief wants to know what you're up to with all of this."

****

I caught Irwin coming out of his office and heading for the stairs. Calling out to him, he doubled back and entered, standing at the side of my desk. I opened my top drawer and pulled out one of the business cards he'd handed me the first day I'd met him. Looking at it, I noted that it said Wright and Wright, Attorneys at Law.

"Is your father named Ulysses?"

He smiled widely, showing his slightly bucked teeth. "That's right. How did you know?"

"Is he still at this address?" I asked, ignoring his question.

The young lawyer nodded his head.

"Okay, that's all I wanted to know."

I stuck the card in my pants pocket and rose from my chair, pushing it closer to the desk, and reached for my hat, which was on the filing cabinet. The little guy looked bewildered, but left without another word, once again heading toward the stairs. I, on the other hand, was going to head out to the parking lot and get in my car and drive on over to 2016 Fort Street—the address on the business card. I needed to see if I could speak with Ulysses Wright about his relationship with Carlo Andolucci. Knowing if the lawyer thought his client was guilty or innocent would make up my mind for me. I'd decide then if I was going to look into this further or not.

Chapter Thirteen

The building at 2016 Fort Street on Detroit's southeast side was a light brown brick structure that loomed five stories. I saw the directory on the wall to the right as soon as I passed through the revolving doors. The attorney's office was on the third floor. Initially, I turned to the right when exiting the elevator, but couldn't locate Suite 311, so I doubled back and went in the opposite direction. It was the second door from the elevator. Looking at the door, I frowned, and then a smile formed on my lips. *Is this guy kidding*? Across the top of the entryway it read, Law Office of U. R. Wright. I shrugged and went in.

Sitting behind a light colored pine desk was a woman of about fifty-five, I was guessing. Her light brown hair was streaked heavily with strands of gray. She was slender and wore dark brown framed glasses and bright orange lipstick. When she spoke, I could see her lipstick had worked its way onto her upper two front teeth.

"Hello, how can I help you?"

"I'm here to see Ulysses Wright," I responded.

She lowered her gaze to an open scheduling book sitting to the right side of her typewriter and asked, "Do you have an appointment?"

"No, uh, no I don't, but I was hoping I could speak to him about something for a few moments anyway. This shouldn't take much of his time."

The woman looked back up at me and shook her head slowly from side to side.

"I doubt that's possible, young man. Mr. Wright doesn't see anyone without an appointment."

"Could you do me a favor and just ask him?"

"He's not here at the moment. He's stepped out."

"When do you expect him back?" I pushed on.

"He should be back anytime, but I'm telling you, he only sees those who've made an appointment. Did you want to make one for another day?"

I shook my head and turned to the chair that was behind me, lowering myself into it.

"No, I'll just take my chances and wait for him if you don't mind."

She shook her head again, as if I was a dummy for not listening to her in the first place.

"Well, suit yourself," she said. "But I'm telling you…."

Not finishing her sentence, she picked up a magazine that had been sitting on her desk, opened to the article she'd been reading. When she lifted the publication, I could see that it was the July 3rd issue of The New Yorker. The cover was red, white, and blue, and had caricatures of men and women, in military uniform, spread out holding hands. As I looked at the cover, Mr. Wright's secretary lifted her eyes to gaze at me over the top of the magazine, and then raised the magazine so I could now see no part of her face whatsoever. I looked around the office. It appeared that Irwin's father didn't do badly for himself. The chair I was sitting in, and an identical one that sat to my left, separated by an expensive looking end table, was made of fine dark brown leather. It was soft and extremely comfortable to sit in. The room was carpeted in plush rust colored wool. On the wall to my right, was a beautifully framed portrait of a young woman dressed in riding britches and holding a crop, standing beside a huge brown stallion. I studied the woman. She was gorgeous with long chestnut waves cascading past her shoulders and her rose colored lips curled in a slight smile. There was something refreshing about her and I wondered if this was someone the attorney knew.

The opening of the door diverted my attention. The man entering *had* to be Irwin's father. He was taller than the young man, but he had the same black hair, parted in the middle and pomaded. He wore glasses, just as Irwin did, and he had the same waxed black mustache. The older gentleman did not share his son's overbite, though. He quickly stepped toward his secretary's desk, laying a long white envelope on it.

"Have there been any calls, Mrs. Volker?"

The woman lowered her magazine and closed it. "No sir," she said, and then nodded toward me.

"Pardon me," the man said after glancing over his shoulder to notice me. "Can I help you?"

"I'm wondering if I can take a few moments of your time," I replied. "I'd like to discuss something with you."

"Do you have an appointment, young man?"

I shook my head. "I'm sure this won't take long, though."

"Can't do it," he said, walking toward the door to his personal office. "I don't see people without an appointment. Mrs. Volker will set one up for you."

And with that, he disappeared behind his heavy oak door, closing it. I glanced at Mrs. Volker, who was looking at me with a smug smirk on her face which said, "I told you so." Immediately, we both looked toward Mr. Wright's inner office. The door had opened and the attorney stuck his head out.

"Get me that file on my next client," he said to his secretary, and then disappeared from sight again, leaving his door ajar.

She only had to extend her left hand to lift it off her desk. The woman rose from her seat and proceeded to walk the way her boss had gone. It was only then that I noticed how tall she was. She had to be five feet ten inches without heels, towering a good inch or two above the man she worked for.

I rose from the chair, deciding not to leave without another attempt at talking to this man. I followed Mrs. Volker, stood just inside his doorway, and cleared my throat. When the secretary looked over her shoulder at me, she wore an expression of surprise that I could be so gutsy. The attorney had been standing behind his desk, bent over, opening the file she'd just laid in front of him. He raised his head to me.

"I'm sorry, but as I told you, you'll have to schedule an appointment for another day. I'm booked solid this afternoon."

"Aren't you Irwin's father?" I asked.

He straightened and removed his glasses. "That's right; what's wrong? Is he in some kind of trouble?"

I held up my right hand, my palm facing the man. "He's fine, nothing like that," I said, trying to put the man's fears to rest immediately.

"Do you know where he is?"

"Yes," I told him. "I saw him earlier at his office."

"He's rented an office?" The elder Mr. Wright asked, somewhat surprised. Then he turned to his secretary and said, "That's fine, Mrs. Volker. You can leave now."

He gestured toward a chair facing his desk and invited me to have a seat. As Mrs. Volker passed me and our eyes met, she could hardly have failed to notice the grin of triumph I wore on my face. I waited until the door closed with her on the other side of it, and then took a seat in one of the overstuffed rust colored chairs which faced the lawyer. Removing my hat, I set it on the seat of the other chair and raised my hands to smooth my hair. Mr. Wright eased himself into his own chair.

"Now what's this about Irwin? He left a few weeks ago and we haven't been in contact. His mother has been worried sick. He didn't leave on such good terms." He then rose from the chair, extending his right hand across the desk. We shook and he sat down again. "I'm Ulysses Wright, and as you know, Irwin's father. And you are?"

"The name is Flanagan, Mr. Wright. Sam Flanagan. I'm a private detective."

Before I could go on, the man lowered his face into both of his hands and sighed loudly. "I knew it! I knew it!" he groaned. "What's the boy done?"

Brief laughter escaped my lips. "Seriously, Mr. Wright, Irwin is fine. He's done nothing as far as I know. He rented the office across from my own on Woodward Avenue and he's setting up shop. He seems to be making some progress; he's hired himself a secretary, and just this morning was having his name painted on his door. I don't think you have anything to worry about."

The man slumped back in his chair and let out a sigh of relief. "I guess I don't give that kid enough credit. That's why he left—he didn't feel I was giving him enough to do, and I guess I wasn't. He said I didn't *trust* him to take anything on, and well...he was right, I didn't. It's just that the courtroom can be a cutthroat place when one isn't used to it and how it's run. It's dog eat dog, Mr. Flanagan. I'm not sure Irwin is going to be able to handle it. I somehow think he's going to get eaten alive out there."

I shrugged. "So what?"

"Huh?"

"I said, so what? He's got to learn the ropes sometime, and he will. You didn't enter law with all the confidence or skill you have now, did you? Maybe you're selling him short. Maybe he'll surprise you one day. You never know."

"Well, that's true," he said, still not convinced. "Okay, so if this isn't about Irwin, why did you come to see me? What did you want to talk to me about?"

I straightened in my chair and got right to the point, telling him about Sophia Andolucci's visit to my office on Saturday afternoon. He'd been Carlo Andolucci's public defender, I'd heard, and I wanted to know his take on the situation.

He frowned. "That was a long time ago, Mr. Flanagan. You say the woman wants to clear her husband's name *now*—after all these *years*?"

I nodded. "That's what she says."

"Hmm," he muttered while pulling at his lower lip. He looked off slightly to his left, focusing at nothing behind my right shoulder. He was deep in thought, recalling something. I gave him another ten seconds to ponder.

"What? What are you thinking?" I asked him.

"I was just remembering," he said. "I'd been a public defender for about four or five years when that case came up. My first job out of law school was in that office. I stayed there all of eight years and then thought 'what the hell am I doing here when I could be making a lot more money working for myself'? So I opened this place." He waved his hand, gesturing around the office space he now rented. "But what strikes me funny is that I recollect him. He'd been down in the city jail for a few days, I think, before I could get to him. We were on a rotation system down at the public defender's office; that's how it works down there. You don't get to pick and choose which cases you'll get. You're assigned them as they come up, and I got this fellow, Andolucci. Well, I knew who he was and I actually didn't want anything to do with it, but what was I going to do? Tell my boss that I was afraid to take the case? I mean, everyone *knew* who he was…who he *worked* for. My wife threw a fit! Irwin was what—eight or nine back then? Anyway, she gave me hell for accepting the case; but like I said, what was I going to do?" He waved his hand dismissively. "Anyway, I go see this guy. It's strange, because as soon as he comes into the room, I tell myself he's been crying." He looked up at me, waiting for my reaction.

"Crying?"

"*Crying*!" he said with emphasis. "His eyes are all red and swollen and watery. I figure the guy's been crying. One of Saperstein's goons is crying like a baby all of a sudden? Just didn't seem to fit. So he sits down across from me and I ask him what happened—tell me all about it, I say to him. I give him time…you know, to pull himself together. I figure the guy can't find his voice. Maybe if he tries to talk, he'll start bawling again. So I wait. And I wait and I wait. The guy doesn't say anything. Finally, I told him if he wanted me to defend him, he had to give me something. Nothing. He doesn't speak. Just stares down at the top of the table sitting between us."

The door to the attorney's inner office opened and Mrs. Volker stuck her head in.

"Your two o'clock appointment is here, Mr. Wright."

"Tell him to wait. I'll be with him in a bit," Wright responded.

She quietly backed out, shutting the door once again.

"He never said anything?" I asked.

"Well, not then, but I went to see him a couple of days later. I ask him all the same questions and he's silent again. Then I finally got a bit angry. I mean, I had never experienced anything like it, and haven't since then. Most people want to get off, or at least make a deal so their sentence will be shortened. Eh, I lost my temper and told him he could find someone else to defend him. Know what he does? He stands up, reaches across the table to shake my hand, and thanks me for my time, and says he hopes he hasn't been too much of an inconvenience to me. Then, he hangs his head, and I can barely make out his words. He says, 'I did it, Mr. Wright.' I mean, this so-called thug is as polite as can be. And I'll tell you what I was thinking as I left the jail that day. I was thinking, 'Hmm, I wonder who he's taking the fall for.' His court date comes up about a month later, and all I can do is stand before the judge with him, entering a plea of guilty. That's it—no contest, no trial. The judge asks him to confirm that that's his plea, and he nods his head and mutters, 'I did it.' Boom…he gets twenty-five to life from the judge. Geez; I mean, what could I do?"

The information Ulysses Wright had just revealed was being absorbed by me. I had a lot to think about and the attorney had a client to see. Picking up my hat, I rose from my chair and thanked him for his time. With my hand on the knob of the door, I turned back at the sound of his voice.

"Hey, Flanagan. So, where is Irwin living now? When he quit here, he moved out of the house as well."

"Now that I can't tell you, because I don't know."

"Well, listen; now that you know where I'm at, how about giving me a call if the boy needs anything…anything at all? You know, like rent money, that sort of thing. Let me know if he gets into trouble in any way, all right?"

I nodded and assured him I would. I had one more question for the man before I exited the office and made my way down to the burgundy Chevy.

"Hey, may I ask who the woman in the portrait is…the one with the horse?"

He smiled widely. "Ah, that was painted years ago. That's my wife…that's Irwin's mother. She rides and has been in several competitions."

The day had been full of surprises for me and I had a huge decision to make. Maybe talking it over with Gran would help me to see things more clearly. It was now twenty minutes past two in the afternoon and there was no reason to head back to the agency. I was going to head home for the day.

CHAPTER FOURTEEN

Gran was standing at the stove in nothing but her slip, turning slices of bacon in a frying pan. I'd just set the kitchen table for the two of us. When I first arrived home, I'd found her slouched in one of the parlor chairs, only dressed in the same slip, snoring loudly. The radio was on, and I knew she'd fallen asleep listening to it. The temperature was eighty-three degrees outside, but there was no breeze circulating in the house and it was terribly humid. When she woke, which was about a half hour ago, she had suggested we have bacon sandwiches along with some cottage cheese for dinner. I was all for it. Number one, I loved bacon, and number two, I didn't want her to spend too much time hovering over a hot stove. Of course, I didn't want to cook, either. She laid the slices of bacon across paper toweling that was on a dinner plate and set it on the table. I'd already placed tomato slices and leaves of lettuce on another plate. Holding the icebox door open, I asked her what she wanted to drink.

"Have I got any beer left, dear?" she asked.

I shook my head. "Nope," I said, feeling guilty because I had drunk it while she was staying at Helen's.

"That's funny. I thought I had a couple in there. Oh well," she shrugged.

Not admitting my transgression, I brought out two bottles of Coca Cola, setting one in front of her, and carried the other back to my seat. We fixed our sandwiches and spooned the cottage cheese onto our plates in silence. As we began to eat, I told her of my day, starting with my call to Mac at the precinct. She listened and I could see reflected in her face that she was taking it all in. She was absorbed; the wheels were turning.

"Hmm," she said.

"What? What are you thinking, Gran?"

"Well, I'm just adding it all up. First you say this man who owns the saloon…what's his name?"

"Neamon Riley," I answered.

"Yes, Mr. Riley. You said he was surprised that this Carlo fellow could do such a thing. Then that other man in the saloon…who was he?"

"A guy named Herschel Sussermann."

"You told me he didn't think that Carlo fit in with all those other crooks. And now the lawyer said he was crying. It's strange, isn't it, dear?"

"What, that a guy who was an enforcer for Saperstein, yet took great strides *not* to hurt anyone and was polite and sensitive, could go into a restaurant full of people and mow them down with a Tommy gun? A guy who was known as The Confessor because he asked for forgiveness with his rosary beads each time he had to rough somebody up? Do I think it's strange that he would think nothing of entering La Bella Luna and kill a handful of innocent people along with the guy who was his initial target? Yeah, Gran, I think it's strange. I think it's real strange."

We continued to eat and while doing so, I noticed my grandmother looking overly tired. Fine beads of sweat played across her forehead, face and upper chest. She seemed drained of energy. Ruby Flanagan wasn't dealing well with this heat and it had me a bit worried.

"Hey, after we finish here, why don't you go sit in a lukewarm bath for a while? I'll clean the kitchen and then head on over to the Stop and Shop and get you a six pack of beer. I need a pack of cigarettes anyway. Maybe we can play some gin rummy later."

"That sounds good, dear. Maybe I will," she said, and then she took a hefty swig of her soda pop.

****

It was seven thirty when I entered the Woodward Avenue building on Wednesday morning. There wasn't a sound coming from any of the other business suites...it appeared I had the place to myself. I pulled out my key, but stopped when I glanced toward Irwin Malcolm Wright's door. Laughter exploded from way deep down inside of me and I put a hand to my chest. I couldn't believe it, but there it was in gold lettering: I. M. Wright Attorney at Law. This was too much!

When I entered my own office, I immediately hauled the Detroit telephone directory out of the top drawer of my filing cabinet. I needed to find a location for Sophia Andolucci. I was determined now to look into this matter, but I wasn't going to do it for free...not as long as she was willing to pay me to do the job I now felt would gnaw at me until I had some concrete answers. Gran asked if I thought the whole thing was strange last night, and I certainly did. It was more than strange. Beginning to feel as Irwin's father had more than nineteen years ago, I wondered who Carlo Andolucci was taking the fall for. Was it someone he cared about and wanted to protect? Or was he ordered by the big boss to take the rap? I wasn't sure, but I wouldn't rest until I knew. The possibility of it still being Andolucci sat at the back of my mind. I just had to delve further into this matter to see if it was a real and viable possibility. Only time would tell, if I was successful in discovering the whole story, that was.

Frustration surfaced within me when I found no Andoluccis in the directory at all. I lifted the receiver of the telephone and dialed the operator, asking her assistance for finding a Sophia Andolucci in the city. Again, I hit a brick wall. With a sudden impulse, I picked up the pencil sitting on my desk and hurled it across the room in anger. Why in the world didn't I get a phone number from her? Why didn't I get her address? I knew why...I hadn't wanted any part of this case when she'd come to see me, and no part of her. The memories she'd shoved in my face...well, I wanted no part of them, either. Now what was I going to do?

"Having a bad day already?"

Startled, I glanced up and saw Frankie Kirkendahl standing in my doorway, leaning against the jamb. She was wearing her deep auburn locks up in a ponytail as I'd seen her wear it yesterday. She wore a mid-calf length, short sleeved, solid navy blue dress that was pulled in snugly at the waist by a wide navy blue belt. I could smell her lavender perfume from where I sat.

"You could say that," I said, running the palm of my hand over my face.

"What's the problem?" she asked, and then said, "Well that's a tough one," after I had told her about my dilemma. "I hope the rest of your day goes better."

She left my vision and walked across the hall, inserting her key into Irwin's office door. Not knowing my next step, I did what I usually did. I headed out, leaving the door behind me opened, to do a little procrastinating. Taking the stairs, I descended onto Woodward Avenue. I was going to go to the nearest diner and get a cup of black coffee to bring back to the office with me. Maybe caffeine would stimulate my brain cells and give me an idea of what to do next.

When I returned, I sat in my swivel chair and looked out the window onto the street below. For the next twenty minutes, I sipped on the java and wondered how I was going to get in touch with Carlo Andolucci's wife. The caffeine I was ingesting had yet to produce any brainstorms. Nothing was coming to mind—nada, zilch, zippo. The sound of movement made me turn my head. It was Frankie again, holding out a piece of paper.

"Here you go. She lives on Bagley in an apartment building. Here's the address. I didn't ask for the phone number. It's Anders now. She changed her name to Anders in the fall of '24."

My face was frozen in a look of complete surprise. *Anders*! I'd forgotten she said she'd changed it!

"How did you know that? How did you ever find her?" I asked, still feeling the jolt of utter amazement.

"I told you, I'm a whiz when it comes to finding things out, but I'll never tell my trade secrets," she replied.

She turned and started to go back to the law office, her heels clicking on the linoleum flooring.

"Wait," I called out. "I might want you to find a couple more names."

"I don't work for you, Mr. Flanagan!" she shouted. "Get your own secretary!"

I heard the door slam from across the hall. Looking down at the address on the paper I now held in my hand, I felt like jumping for joy; but instead, I grabbed my hat and keys.

****

The Harrington Arms apartment complex sat in the middle of a residential section on Bagley Avenue. The exterior of the two-story building was red brick. It had a double glass entryway, a buzzer, along with the occupants' names, to the right of it. It appeared that an S. Anders lived in apartment 224. I rang the buzzer, waited a full minute, and then rang it again. A winded voice talked to me through the intercom.

"Yes?"

"Is this Sophia Anders? This is Sam Flanagan," I said.

There was hesitation, and then, "Flanagan? The detective?"

"Yes, Sophia, may I come in?"

She hesitated a few more seconds and then I heard the buzz of the lock unlatching. I grabbed the knob and entered. Climbing the stairs two at a time, I found the woman standing in the hallway, awaiting my arrival. When I reached her, she motioned with her hand for me to enter. Her apartment was spacious and clean, but the furniture gracing the parlor room was threadbare. It seemed I'd caught her just coming out of the shower, as she wore a tattered robe and had her damp, black hair wrapped up in a towel. The lady still looked tired and worn out.

"May I sit down?" I asked as soon as she closed the door.

She said nothing, but gestured to a chair that faced the sofa. I moved to it and lowered myself into the seat, but she remained standing, her arms folded across her chest. She hadn't said anything since I'd arrived, and I now felt the defiance in her stance. With my brown fedora in hand, I motioned toward the couch.

"You may want to sit down, too," I suggested.

"What for? I have to be at work in an hour, Mr. Flanagan. I can hear what you have to say just fine from where I stand. What do you want?"

This woman was angry. She was bitter about my having as good as kicked her out of my office four days ago when she had come begging for my help.

I sighed and said, "Because I want you to tell me about your husband; that is, if you still want me to take the case, and if you have the time."

I was praying she would say yes. Either way, I was going to pursue this now; it's just that I wanted to get paid for my time and effort.

"What do you want to know about him?" she asked after sighing heavily.

"Specifically, what makes you feel he was innocent of the La Bella Luna shootings?"

She sighed again. "I *told* you; he was with me at the time."

The lady was still standing. I didn't want this to be turned into a session of me working this hard to pull all the information out of her.

"Listen, I know you're upset about the other day, but I'm here now and I'm willing to listen. Can you thaw out a little bit? It would make this go a lot easier."

Reluctantly, she backed up and eased herself down onto the sofa. She crossed her legs and straightened her robe, making sure that her knee wasn't showing. In a small voice, Sophia Andolucci told me again of how, at the age of seventeen, she and her brother, Nito, made their way to the United States from Librizzi, Sicily, and how a letter had arrived from her uncle shortly thereafter. In it, he'd requested that she befriend his godson, Carlo, who was on his own voyage to the country she now called home. They'd hit if off immediately, even though there was an age difference of twelve years. The two became inseparable and five months later, they were married.

"He found employment right away," she said. "I'm not stupid, Mr. Flanagan, I knew who he worked for. One didn't live in this city without knowing who ran it back then. But I never really knew exactly what he did. I didn't ask, and Carlo never really spoke of it. We were happy, so what did it matter?"

"What did it matter?"

I couldn't help it; the question just spewed from my mouth in a venomous tone. Surprised, she glanced up and her eyes met mine. I shook my head.

"Never mind," I said. "Go on."

"We'd been married a little over a year and a half when I found I was expecting Carlo Jr. In those first months, I hadn't been feeling so well. That night…the night of the murders…Carlo stayed with me. I'd eaten very little that day and couldn't keep anything down. I knew this was normal, but Carlo was so worried. He was such a gentle, caring man."

I found myself getting angry inside. *A gentle, caring man*? I tried to push aside my disgust as she continued speaking.

"He was almost like a father to Nito, but now he was going to become a real father. He was so excited about the baby. I guess I was really like a mother to Nito myself. I suppose we sort of acted like his parents, guiding him, protecting him. But now we would have a child of our own. We were so happy."

Her face took on a look of sadness and I realized that, having not even lived with the man for almost twenty years, she was still very much in love with him.

"Did he stay with you that whole night?" I asked.

"No, there was one period when he left. He'd called the doctor and told him of my nausea. The doctor called in a prescription for some type of tonic to settle my stomach. Carlo left me briefly to go to Cunningham's Drugstore on

Grand River to pick it up. He wasn't gone more than a half hour, and that was about four thirty in the afternoon. They were getting ready to close for the day."

Her face took on a look of pleading, and she leaned forward in her seat.

"Don't you see? He was here with me when that occurred at the restaurant!"

I began to calculate the time mentally.

"You say he was back by five o'clock?"

"Yes," she said. "Or just a few minutes after."

If she was telling the truth—and why would she come out with a lie at this stage? —her husband wasn't anywhere near La Bella Luna at the time of the shootings. I had learned years ago that the incident happened around five thirty on that Thursday evening in April.

"I only ask that you look into it, Mr. Flanagan; that is, if you're finished with whatever other case it was that you were working on."

I said nothing, but sat staring at the fedora in my hands, pondering the possibility that I had been mistaken all these years as to the identity of my father's killer. Had we all believed a lie? And if so, why was it that Carlo Andolucci, himself, had wanted us to believe it?

My thoughts were interrupted by the arrival of a man who entered through the front door of the apartment. He probably stood just less than six feet tall and appeared solid and muscular under the work coveralls he wore. His hair was dark and was shaved very short, high above his ears. The coloring of his skin was a deep, golden tan from sun exposure. I was guessing he did some type of work outdoors. I could see a fine chain hanging from his neck and tucked inside his clothing. He wore a large gold ring with a small diamond on his right hand.

"Hey," he said. "I thought I was taking you to work today. What gives?" And then he caught sight of me. He frowned when he looked my way. "Who the hell is this, Sophia?"

She introduced us, telling me this was her brother, Nito. I rose and extended my hand, but he refused it.

"A peeper? You hired a damn peeper?" He turned toward her. "What did I tell you? All this guy's gonna do is steal your money! What's he gonna find out after so many years? I told you you're wasting your time and money; let it go!"

His sister rubbed her forehead and sighed. "Nito, please! You know how I feel. I want this for young Carlo and I want this for me, too. I want this settled once and for all. Just let me do as I wish. There's coffee on the stove. Just leave me to this."

He turned back to me, gave me a dirty look, and shook his head. He then proceeded to walk in the direction of the kitchen.

Sophia rose and asked what my fee was. When I told her it was ten dollars a day, she told me to wait. When she left the room, I glanced at the mantle above the small fireplace that sat across the room from me. It had a few knick knacks sitting on top of it, along with two photos in silver frames. I moved forward to get a better look. In the one, a young man of about thirty years of age was standing outside, leaning against his automobile...a tan 1920 Buick. His hair was black and combed straight back away from his face, which was clean shaven. His suit, a black pin stripe, looked expensive. He was smiling in the photo and he was quite handsome. I picked up the photo next to it. This one was of a younger fellow, maybe sixteen or seventeen years old. Carlo and Carlo Jr., I guessed.

If I was right in assuming who they were, Carlo Jr. was the spitting image of his father.

Sophia reentered the room, took the picture of her son from my hands, and replaced it on the shelf.

"Your son?" I asked.

She nodded and handed me some bills she had in her hands. I counted it out in front of her; fifty dollars.

"Will that be enough to at least get you started, Mr. Flanagan?"

"This'll do."

****

With the window rolled all the way down, I sat in the Chevy, which was parked across the street and over a few doors from the Harrington Arms. Puffing on a Lucky Strike, I was thinking of all I had learned in the last few days. As Gran had tried to do last night, I was adding it all up. Ten minutes had passed when I saw Sophia and Nito exit her building and enter a 1937 black Chrysler Imperial that had been parked out front at the curb. Nito started the engine and pulled slowly out onto Bagley. As he passed me, our eyes met. He was still wearing a scowl. A few minutes later, I, too, pulled out. The Cunningham Drugstore over on Grand River Avenue was my destination.

Chapter Fifteen

It felt good inside the pharmacy. Overhead fans cooled the air and created a soft breeze. I walked straight to the counter, where a heavy-set woman in her fifties was paying for items; a bottle of Anacin aspirin tablets, a large container of Kolynos tooth powder, a jar of Vicks VapoRub, and four chocolate bars. The man behind the counter, ringing up her purchases, looked to be in his early thirties. His hair was a light brown, frizzing on top, but worn short. Freckles covered his face and spread across his forehead and into his hairline. He wore a clean, white lab coat. I assumed he was the druggist, but I knew he couldn't have been employed here twenty years ago because of his young age.

"Can I help you, sir?" he asked when the woman headed for the door, bag in hand.

I stepped up closer and leaned on the surface of the counter with my right forearm.

"Yeah, I'd like to ask you for some information. I am sure you weren't working here nineteen or twenty years ago—"

His laugh interrupted me.

"No sir, you'd be correct. Twenty years ago I would've been in the seventh grade, trying not to fall asleep during history class."

"Well, I was wondering if you could tell me who the pharmacist was back then. I know it's a long shot, but would you happen to know?"

"Sure, that would be Mr. Hollister."

"Know where I can find this Mr. Hollister?" I asked.

He nodded. "Of course," he said. Then he gestured with his head to his right. "He's in the back room."

I straightened. "You mean he still works here?"

"Yep, he's what you might call the senior pharmacist. Been working here for ages."

"Think I might be able to speak to him?" I asked, feeling like one lucky son of a gun.

"I don't see why not; but I suppose I should let him answer that."

He turned away from me and entered a door which was to his right, disappearing behind it. The man who emerged from the same door was maybe five feet ten inches tall and on the portly side. His gray hair was longer than what I'd expected it to be, and it stuck out in different directions. The gold wire-rimmed glasses he wore sat at an angle across the bridge of his nose. My instant impression was one of a mad scientist.

"You wanted to speak to me, mister?"

"Yes," I answered. "The other fellow said you worked here twenty years ago."

"Well, that's only partly true. Come October, I'll have been here forty-one years."

Before I could respond, he let go of a belly laugh. "Hehehe, I know what you're thinking. You're thinking there's no way that man is sixty-six years old; am I right?"

I was actually thinking he looked to be in his early seventies, but I played the game and said, "Wow, that's right!

I figured you to be more like fifty, but working here for forty-one years rules that one out!"

He laughed again. "Hehehe, I assume most people think that. Now, what is it you wanted to speak to me about?"

"Between nineteen and twenty years ago, a man came in here to pick up a prescription you had orders to fill from his wife's doctor. His name was Carlo Andolucci. She was pregnant at the time and feeling nauseous. He came in around closing time. This was on Thursday, April 24, 1924. Do you recollect any of that?"

He looked at me with his eyebrows furrowed.

"You've got to be kidding me! You expect me to remember who comes in for a prescription over nineteen years ago? I couldn't tell you who came in a month ago, let alone back in 1924!"

"Well, I knew it would be one chance in a million that you'd remember," I admitted. "It's just that this particular guy confessed to the La Bella Luna shootings the next day. That would've placed him at the restaurant soon after he left here. I was trying to confirm he was here and what time."

"I *do* remember that incident, but I couldn't tell you if the guy was in here or not right before he mowed those people down. Hell, I couldn't even tell you when that happened. Years ago, I know. But I can tell you this; Arthur Nass was in that restaurant at the time of the shootings. He was there with his wife and his parents."

"Who?"

"Arthur Nass. Nice fella. He comes in here every now and then."

"Do you have a home address for this Arthur Nass?" I asked him.

He nodded his head. "I do, but *you're* not going to get it. I don't give out my customers' addresses. But he owns the butcher shop a few doors down." He pointed in which direction.

Before leaving the pharmacy, I thanked him and told him he'd been a big help.

"Anytime, mister."

I headed for the door, but stopped just short of it, noticing the scale to the right. For a penny, I could weigh myself and get my fortune told. I hopped on and inserted the coin. Two hundred and eight pounds, it read. I waited for the machine to spit out what awaited me in the future. "You will receive word that a long lost uncle wants to bestow an inheritance of vast sums upon you." I laughed and tossed the slip of paper into the trash can sitting by the exit.

****

When I entered the butcher shop on Grand River Avenue, I found the place virtually empty of customers. A man in a white coat stood behind the counter, bent over, positioning a tray of chicken legs inside the display. He looked up when I walked through the door.

"Good morning," he called out.

"Howdy," I nodded, walking casually toward him, my hands inside my trouser pockets.

"What can I help you with? Whole chickens are on sale for twenty-two cents a pound today."

"Are you Arthur Nass?" I asked, initially ignoring his question.

He said nothing, but nodded his head. Then I spied the ring of bologna on the countertop behind him.

"Uh, give me a dime's worth of that," I said, pointing to it. "I'll take a dime's worth of the cheese, too, and throw in a handful of crackers."

He turned to slice the bologna. Mr. Nass was probably not more than five years older than me, with sandy colored hair that was neat and parted on the side. His light blue eyes highlighted a friendly face.

"I actually want to ask you a few questions if you don't mind," I said.

"Sure, about what?" he asked over his right shoulder.

"About what happened at La Bella Luna years ago."

His head and shoulders pivoted fully till he was looking me straight on, holding my gaze. Then he turned back and continued what he was doing.

"Why do you want to know about that?" he asked. When he was finished, he handed me my package, saying, "That'll be twenty-three cents." I paid the man and then he motioned for me to follow him. "Come on in the break room." But before he came out from behind his display, he opened a door leading to the back of the business, "Hey, Eddie, watch the front for me for a few minutes, will ya?"

I followed the butcher down a short, narrow hallway and into a tiny room which sat to the left. Inside was a small table, two chairs against the ends of it. On the table sat half-filled salt and pepper shakers. The room also held an icebox that stood near a countertop with a sink in the middle of it. A metal thermos sat on the counter.

He gestured for me to sit at the table, and I did. Arthur Nass reached for the thermos and held it out to me.

"Want some coffee?"

I shook my head no and he proceeded to unscrew the top of it, pouring the black drink into the makeshift cup. When he sat down, I asked him to tell me what he'd observed that day in April over nineteen years ago.

"First of all," he said. "Who are you and what's your interest in all of this?"

I told him who I was and why I wanted his account of the situation.

"It's something I'm never gonna forget, I can tell you that. April 24th is my wife's birthday. We'd only been married a couple of years and I decided to take her out to dinner as a celebration. We asked Ma and Dad to go with us. We'd only been there about fifteen minutes before all hell broke loose. I was facing the door and I spotted the gun right away. I guess I yelled out 'Get down!'...at least that's what my wife says. It all happened so fast. Anyway, we were all lucky enough to dive under the table without getting hit. But there were some who weren't so lucky."

I was all too aware of that.

"What did this guy look like, Mr. Nass?"

"It happened all too quick, like I said. He had a hat pulled down over his face, but I could tell he had real dark hair. I don't know. But the guy who did it confessed. Some guy who worked for Abe Saperstein."

"Did he say anything before he opened fire? Do you remember?"

"Nope, not that I recall. He just came through the door and started killing people. I remember thinking as he entered, for just a split second...it's like he didn't belong there. I think it was his clothes. Yeah, that's it. La Bella Luna was a fancy place. Hell, I saved for a couple of months to be able to buy Rita and my folks dinner there. And this guy comes in dressed in denim pants and sneakers. He didn't seem to fit. I remember that. And then I noticed the gun."

He took a sip of his coffee as I was mulling over what he'd just told me.

"When the shooting stopped, what did he do then?"

"I guess he ran out of the restaurant."

"Why do you think that?" I asked him.

"Because I remember hearing the door open right after the bullets stopped flying. I looked up from under the table and didn't see him anymore. He was gone and people were crying and moaning."

****

Sitting on a bench in a nearby park, I ate my bologna and cheese on crackers under the sweltering summer sun. Arthur Nass hadn't told me much, but what he did tell me spoke volumes. If what he remembered was accurate, the man in the denim trousers and sneakers didn't seem to fit the image of Carlo Andolucci, snazzy dresser that he was. The man who hastily made his getaway from the scene of carnage didn't fit Carlo "The Confessor" Andolucci's modus operandi. Of what I'd heard from Neamon Riley, word on the street had it that the enforcer belonging to the Purple Gang always pulled out a string of rosary beads and asked for forgiveness after a dirty deed had been done. If Carlo Andolucci had committed this crime, why change his pattern now? Surely this was the mother of all crimes in the face of God. Surely amends would have to be made between the man and his Maker. I wasn't completely ruling out that it was Carlo Andolucci in La Bella Luna, but the more I learned of that fateful day, the more I felt it was *not* he who had killed my father and wounded my mother.

Done with my snack, I looked at my watch. It was going on 11:30 a.m. I rose and brushed crumbs from my navy blue trousers and headed for the Chevy parked at the curb. There were people to try to locate and the day was young.

Chapter Sixteen

My next stop was to a branch of the local public library. When I entered, I saw a group of about ten or twelve youngsters ranging in age from seven to ten seated in a semi-circle on the carpeted floor, listening to a story being read by a young librarian. For the most part, the children were engulfed in the tale. But I noticed one little boy looking around, his thumb in his mouth, his other hand holding onto a waft of his hair, twirling it. He caught my eye and I smiled.

An older librarian was behind the main desk and I asked her assistance in looking through the newspaper archives. She directed me to a separate room and helped me locate the April 25, 1924 issue of the Detroit News. It took me all of five minutes to read the account twice. The names of the victims were included in the brief article, the name Connor Flanagan jumping at me from the page, and I felt a stab of sadness and pain. I'd confirmed what I thought I knew. The shooting took place at 5:33 p.m. on the evening of the twenty-fourth. I then asked her if they carried a telephone directory, and she pulled one out from below the counter at her station at the desk. I thumbed through it and found what I was looking for. Mario Nardini resided at 23340 Adelaide Street. Hmm, that was a very nice area in the city. I then found a K. Nelson living in the Somerset Apartments on the corner of Dubois and Jefferson. Jotting the information down in the little black book I carried in my top shirt pocket, I'd felt elated that my mission had been accomplished.

****

The house on Adelaide was a sprawling three-story Tudor style. The structure was protected on all sides by a high, brown brick barricade. A double wrought iron gate sat as the entryway into the front yard. I parked directly across from the home and got out of the auto. Walking up to the gate, I suddenly noticed the two men standing near the door to the home. Both were smoking cigarettes, and both wore shoulder holsters holding Smith and Wesson .22's over their short sleeved shirts. When I reached the gate, I tried to open it, but it was locked. That's when the men noticed me. The taller of the two stamped his cigarette out on the pavement near the small porch with the toe of his shiny black shoe, and then meandered toward me.

"Yeah?" he asked.

"I want to see Mario Nardini," I answered him.

"You got an appointment with him?"

"No, I don't."

"Well, you ain't seein' him then," he said in a not too friendly tone of voice.

"Why don't you let him decide that?" I suggested. "Tell him Sam Flanagan wants to talk to him."

The guy looked at me from head to toe. The deep scar along his right temple started to twitch. He smiled and looked back at his buddy. He gave a little laugh and gestured toward me with a thumb.

"Hey, Rico; we got a big-shot here." He then turned to face me once again. "I don't think you're hearin' me, pal. You ain't seein' nobody here today, capiche?"

Beyond this guy, I could see Rico put his hand on top of the holstered gun while he took a deep drag off his cigarette. Our eyes met and held for ten seconds. I looked at the one standing right in front of me again.

"You just tell your boss that Sam Flanagan was here and wants to talk to him, so I'll be back. Capiche?"

"Yeah, pal; I'll try to remember that."

He stood right where he was until I'd crossed the street and entered the Chevy. I reached in my pocket for a Lucky Strike. I lit it and looked back at the gate. He was still eying me. It wasn't until I started the car and eased away from the curb that I saw him turn and slowly walk back to Rico.

Well, I'd bombed out on that one, but my less than welcome reception made me all the more determined to get in there to speak to Nardini. It might take me awhile to come up with an idea on how to gain entrance, but I would come up with something. In the meantime, I wanted to go home and take a cold shower. The sun was pounding down with a vengeance. The sky was a deep blue and clear of any clouds. The temperature was approaching ninety. I kept thinking about how Gran was listless last night during dinner and I was a bit concerned about her. I needed to check up on her...but first, I'd make my way over to the Somerset Apartments.

****

Four young boys were shooting marbles on the sidewalk in front of the four-story brown wood-frame apartment building. I had to walk around them to reach the concrete steps leading to the door. I found no directory at the door, or inside in the small foyer, but I'd written down Kate Nelson's apartment number while I was at the library. She lived on the third floor in apartment 33C. By the time I reached it, I was a tad winded because of the heat; there was no elevator in this building and I'd had to climb the two flights of stairs. I felt the sweat roll down the sides of my cheeks and wiped my face using the back of my hand. The apartment I wanted was almost down the full length of the hall and on the right. As I approached, I heard music coming from the other side of the door. Good, at least I'd find the woman at home. I gave a loud rap and then waited. The apartment went silent; the music had been turned off. I waited a full minute more before I decided to knock a second time. The door was jerked open a few seconds later.

The woman who stood just inside the apartment had her hand on the edge of the door above her head. She looked me up and down.

"Yeah?" she asked in a voice that was a bit chilly.

"Are you Kate Nelson?"

"And just who wants to know?" she asked, and then let go of an almost silent belch.

The smell of cheap gin made its way toward my nostrils. She was dressed in black lingerie; a long silk gown and matching robe that was left open. She wore nothing on her feet except bright red nail polish, which matched her perfectly painted fingernails. Her bosom was ample and its cleavage was staring at me—I couldn't *help* but notice. She was probably somewhere in her mid-forties, with soft lines at the corners of her brown eyes. Her hair was dark and curved under slightly right below her earlobes. Across her forehead, full bangs fell straight. She wore a silky black band on her head with the tied ends coming around from the nape of her neck to lie against the front of her left shoulder. Her pink lipstick was a bit smudged, but all in all, she was rather attractive.

"The name is Sam Flanagan. I..."

"Oh, for God's sake, don't tell me! He's dead, isn't he? Are you his lawyer?"

"Who's dead?"

"Sid? Is Sid Buczynski dead?"

"I don't know a Sid Buczynski. I'm here to talk to you about another man you know, or at least used to know. Abe Saperstein."

"Oh," she said, sounding disappointed. "Come another day," she continued as she put her left hand to her stomach. "I'm not feeling too well today." And then she closed the door in my face.

I stood there staring at the barrier between her and myself. She'd slammed the door on me, and I couldn't help but wonder if her disappointment stemmed from the fact that I'd mentioned Abe Saperstein, or if it was because Sid Buczynski wasn't dead.

Turning away, I headed for the stairs. Very soon I would knock on her door again, but right now, I wanted to get home to check on my grandmother.

CHAPTER SEVENTEEN

Gran was sitting in the front parlor in her slip, a brand new Delco floor model fan blowing on her. The head of the fan rotated from side to side, providing a cool airflow throughout the room. We'd had a smaller version, but the motor had burnt out this year in the middle of June. I smiled when I looked at the new addition.

"Hey, where'd you get it?" I asked, pointing to the fan.

"Mae Randle said she was going to Montgomery Ward in Dearborn this morning and I asked if I could go along with her."

Mae Randle was the mother of Albie and Bobby next door.

"Where'd you get the money for it?"

"From your top drawer, dear," my grandmother answered. "It was seven dollars and ninety-five cents, and then I bought us a sandwich and a root beer at the lunch counter. It was the least I could do since she was nice enough to take me along with her."

"I only had twelve dollars in there. Do I have any left?"

She shook her head. "Nope, I bought myself this new slip, too, along with some chocolates."

I looked on the end table near her. A small box which used to contain a half dozen or so pieces of milk chocolate was now open and empty. Normally, this might have irritated me just a tad, but I had the fifty big ones in my pocket that Sophia Anders, Andolucci—whatever she wanted to call herself these days—had given me this morning. And quite honestly, I felt the money was well spent. We both needed some way to keep cool in this summer swelter. Despite the fan providing her relief from the heat, Gran sat slumped against the back of the chair and appeared listless.

"Are you feeling all right?" I asked.

She nodded and then said, without looking at me, "There's a leak in the bathroom sink, dear."

I made my way to the bedroom and took my shirt off, leaving only my sleeveless undershirt to cover my chest. Heading out to the garage in the back, I got my tool box and brought it into the house. I'd take care of the leak and then I'd take that shower that I'd been thinking of. Entering the bathroom, I found Shamus standing on the edge of the sink, his head lowered just below the faucet, lapping up the cold drips of water as they formed. He meowed loudly when I scooped him up and gently placed him on the floor. The cat then jumped right back to where he'd been, waiting for the next droplet of moisture to appear. Again, I took him in my hands, but carried him into the kitchen before I returned to the bathroom, shutting the door behind me.

Forty-five minutes later found the sink with a new washer and me standing under a spray of tepid water in the tub. Feeling the moisture cover my body, I allowed myself to think of nothing. Tomorrow would be another day. For the rest of today, I didn't want to even think of Carlo Andolucci or any other player that could've been involved in the La Bella Luna shootings.

But that wasn't to be. As soon as I emerged from the bathroom, Gran wanted me to sit with her in the front room and tell her all about my day; if I had made any progress. I filled her in on my visit to Sophia Andolucci's, my talk with the pharmacist and butcher, and ended by telling her how I was unsuccessful in gaining access to speak to either Mario Nardini or Kate Nelson. She sat quietly and listened, not interrupting me once. When I was through, she nodded and sighed, but said nothing.

"Hey, are you sure you're okay? Something's wrong, I know it."

"I don't know," she said. I saw her bottom lip quiver slightly and then I thought I knew what might be bothering her.

"Have you talked to Helen since you've been home?" I asked.

She shook her head and I could see her eyes beginning to water. That bottom lip was trembling again. Helen and my grandmother had been friends for as long as I could remember. Gran had walked away from Helen's house and Helen didn't even have the courtesy to call and find out if she was home or not. I could see how that would hurt my grandmother very deeply. I slapped my knees with the opened palms of my hands and stood up.

"Hey, I've got an idea! Let's go out for supper. It's too hot to cook and it will do us good to get out for a bit. What do you say?"

Ruby Flanagan lifted her eyes to mine and I saw a bit of life flicker in her face.

"You mean it?" she asked.

"Of course, I do. We can go wherever you want," I said.

****

I was back on Woodward Avenue, about four blocks away from my office. I pulled up and parked at the curb across the street from the restaurant my grandmother had told me she wanted to try—it was a "new place" she had told me, one that had just opened a few weeks ago. When I emerged from the Chevy, I looked up at the sign that was above the green and white striped canvas awning that hung over the door of the business. A whistle escaped my lips, and I shoved my fedora slightly back on my head.

"You're kidding me, right?"

Gran shook her head and giggled. "He's going to be so surprised to see us!"

We crossed the street and entered "Augie's Cuchina." The interior smelled of spicy sausage, onions, tomatoes, and oregano. It wasn't a large restaurant, but it smacked of warmth and coziness with its five round tables sitting in the middle and six high-backed booths positioned along the wall. Each table was covered in a green and white checkered cloth, small containers of Italian spices placed in the middle. The flooring was shiny, dark green linoleum. Three overhead fans rotated constantly to create a comfortable atmosphere, while soft violin music was piped into the space to provide a soothing and relaxing experience for diners. I was quite impressed…who knew Augie had it in him?

I'd met Augie back in January of this year. He was a bodyguard of sorts and driver for a client of mine. She lived in Chicago and was high-society. After I was finished with my case and returned home, I had learned he'd cut ties with his life in the Windy City and come back to the Detroit area also, where he had been born and raised, moving back into his parents' home. The guy was an enigma to me, hardly saying anything at all in my presence; but apparently he had a great fondness for my grandmother, visiting her often–in my absence, of course.

A man of about thirty-five met us at the door with menus in his hand. His ebony hair was combed to one side and he was clean shaven. He smiled, forming dimples in his cheeks.

"You two want a table or a booth?" he inquired.

"Oh, a booth, please!" my grandmother said with excitement.

I removed the fedora from my head as she and I followed the man to the very back of the restaurant. He gestured to a booth which was right across from the swinging louvered doors leading into the kitchen. On route, I noticed two other booths were occupied, as well as one table. We took our seats facing each other and I noticed the girlish grin on Gran's face as she looked around in awe at her surroundings. She glanced toward the kitchen and spied Augie, who wore a white apron draped around his neck. Gran waved and called out to him. The big guy smiled and waved back. Then he caught sight of me and turned around to resume what he'd been doing.

"My name is Dominic Consiglio, and I'll be your waiter. You know my brother, Augustino?" he asked as he handed us each a menu.

"Augie's your brother?"

He looked at me and nodded. "Yeah, he's my baby brother."

"Yes, we know him," Gran said.

The man smiled and asked, "Want me to get you some wine?"

"Why not? Bring us each a glass…something you would recommend, Dominic," I told him.

"What were you thinking of having tonight?"

"Pizza," Gran blurted out. "Can we get a pizza, Sam?"

I took the menu from my grandmother and handed them both to Augie's brother. "Pizza it is then."

Two minutes later, we each had a large wine glass half filled with Chianti. We'd been told by Dominic that "it goes good with pizza." I took a sip and sat back in the booth, noticing the occupants of the table in the middle of the restaurant. Four ladies, who seemed to be of college age, were staring at me and giggling softly. I wondered what was so funny, but then started to relax as the one girl smiled widely and lowered her eyes shyly.

"So, don't you think this is a nice little restaurant, dear?" Gran asked.

"Yeah, it's all right at that. You didn't tell me Augie opened this place."

My grandmother shrugged while reaching for her wine. "I guess I didn't think of it. He's been talking about it for quite a while now."

I frowned. "Just how often do you see this guy?"

"Oh, I don't know; enough, I suppose. He visited a week ago Sunday…that night you went to listen to your friend, Hep Cat, play music in his garage. We played some hands of poker," she said. Gran took a sip of wine and made a face at the bitter taste of it. "He won seventy-four cents from me that night," she said.

"*You* played poker? For *money*?" I laughed at the thought of it, and then asked with my eyebrows furrowed, "Where'd you get the money?"

"Your top drawer, dear."

Suddenly, my amusement was gone. Something told me I was going to have to find a new place to store my moolah. At the rate my grandmother spent my bills and loose change, I would never be able to save anything. Another option would be to give her a small allowance of her own each week, but I'd have to mull that one over.

It wasn't long before a silver platter holding the pizza was set in the middle of the table. The pie was thick with pepperoni, mushrooms, onions, green pepper, and mozzarella on top. Dominic placed a white ceramic plate in front of each of us and began to cut the pizza into wedges, then transferred a piece onto each of our plates. He bowed while saying "Enjoy," but what he did next surprised me somewhat. He pulled a chair over from one of the vacant tables and placed the back of it up to the end of our booth. He then straddled it, joining us while we ate. With his arms resting on the back of the chair, he eyed the pizza.

"Would you like a piece?" Gran asked him.

"I don't mind if I do," was his answer. He reached out and scooped up a wedge with both hands. "So, how do you know Augie?" he asked.

Gran dove right in, telling him about my trip to Chicago and the case I'd been working on. I was only half listening until I caught the eye of the young lady at the table once again. Then I stopped listening altogether. She continued to watch me, smiling. For an instant, I thought I saw her wink, but I couldn't be sure. I smiled back and gave a little wave. She and her friends began to snicker softly again—and then she blew me a kiss. *Ah, you must still have it, even at forty, Flanagan;* I thought to myself. We played goo-goo eyes with each other for a few more minutes while I ate. My attention was drawn away when Dominic suddenly rose from the chair and went to the door leading back into the kitchen.

"Hey, Augie, get on out here for a minute," he said loudly.

I looked at Gran questioningly. She shrugged while chewing her food. Dominic returned to his chair. He looked at me and said, "I think my brother can help you with that."

I was confused. "Help me with what?"

"Getting in to see Mario," he replied.

Mario? Was he talking about Mario Nardini? I glanced at Gran and wondered what in the world she'd been telling the man. I wasn't sure I liked her discussing the cases I was working on at present with people we didn't know. My lips drew taut, allowing her to be aware of my disappointment, and she shrugged again.

"HEY AUGIE!" the man yelled over his left shoulder. "COME HERE!"

He was so loud I jumped slightly in the booth, and the other diners looked our way.

Dominic Consiglio turned back to us, shaking his head. "Eh, that's all he does is stay in that kitchen, baking. This is his business and we're helping him out, but I work construction and I can't stay here forever. If he's going to make it, he's got to make it on his own. He's got Mama in the kitchen with him, and Angelo does the books. I guess some wacky old broad taught him how to make peanut butter cookies, and he does nothing else with his time here."

I straightened in my seat—peanut butter cookies? I was a sucker for peanut butter cookies, and the idea of taking a half dozen home with us formed in my mind.

Gran perked up and smiled. "That was me!" she said, and blushed.

Dominic seemed stunned for an instant and then recovered nicely by switching to charming mode and laying it on thick. The man grabbed my grandmother's hand and kissed it.

"Now Augie never told us that his baking teacher was so youthful looking and delightful."

Gran turned a deeper shade of crimson and fluttered her eyelids while grinning shyly. I rolled my eyes. What was worse? A guy who only grunted in my presence, or his brother, Dominic, who was a Casanova, falsely flattering old women?

"AUGIE!" he shouted for a third time.

Finally, the big lug strolled out of the kitchen—all four-hundred pounds of him. He came up to the booth and just stood there, saying nothing. Dominic gestured with his thumb in my direction.

"You need to take your friend here over to see Uncle Mario. He needs to talk to him," he said to his brother.

Uncle Mario?

"Mario Nardini is your *uncle*?" I asked in astonishment.

"Well, no, not really. We call him that, though," Dominic said. "He's Augie's godfather."

CHAPTER EIGHTEEN

Augustino Consiglio had agreed to meet me the next day at two o'clock in the afternoon at his godfather's home. As I lay in bed, I thought of what luck I'd been having in this case. It certainly was a small world! I was hopped up by the fact that I wouldn't have to come up with a scheme to worm my way in to see the old man who had been Abe Saperstein's partner in crime.

Even though I was relieved of this problem, sleep eluded me. Gran and I had both called it an early night, crawling into bed by nine thirty. I'd fallen asleep moments later, but woke again for some reason. It was the heat, it had to be. My window was fully opened, but the air that lingered directly outside was motionless and humid. The bedside clock told me it was twenty-two minutes to midnight.

I sat up on the edge of the bed and rubbed the back of my neck, which was covered in a fine layer of sticky perspiration. I leaned forward and to my left, placing my face near the screen of the window, and looked out. No breath of air touched me.

Getting out of bed, I made my way to the kitchen for a glass of water to bring back to my room. Passing Gran's door, I could hear her snores above the soft whirring noise of the new fan that was positioned in her room to blow air onto her so she could sleep. At least I was at ease knowing she was comfortable. This heat had been miserable and I longed for a break from the high temperatures. Back in my room, I propped a couple of pillows against my headboard and kicked the bedspread and sheet to the foot of the bed. While smoking a cigarette in the dark, I thought of the day my sister, Eva, had gotten married; a day which was supposed to be the happiest of her life; a day in which she couldn't hide the sadness on her face. It must have been almost two o'clock in the morning before I closed my eyes again and drifted off.

****

On Thursday morning, by 10:00 a.m., I was on my way back to the Somerset Apartments. It was July 8. I bypassed breakfast, coffee, and going into the office, wanting to talk to Kate Nelson before my appointment with Augie at the house on Adelaide. I was hoping she was up for the day, and I was hoping she'd be sober and in more of a receptive mood. When I reached the third floor, there was a man down the corridor, holding a brown grocery bag and fumbling with his keys, attempting to enter an apartment. The bag was dangerously close to falling from his grasp. I hurried forward to assist him, and got there just in time to save his groceries from slipping to the floor.

"Hey, thanks, buddy. I got eggs in there, and the little lady would kill me if they ended up all over the floor out here."

"Not a problem," I said.

This man was probably in his mid-fifties, I was guessing. The top of his head was bare of any hair, but there was a thick amount spanning from ear to ear. He wore belted tan trousers with a yellowing short sleeved undershirt tucked in them. The shirt was stained and wet under his armpits. He was short and pudgy around the middle, and for some reason, I thought of a toad while looking at him.

"Hey, you the guy who's gonna rent 37C?" He extended his hand. "If so, I'll be your neighbor. This here is me and my wife's place. The name's Rogers; Jason and Janet Rogers."

"No," I said while shaking his hand. "Not me. I'm just here to see a friend." I nodded to 33C across the hall.

"Ah," he said. "Miss Nelson? Nice lady, but she generally keeps to herself. Doesn't have many visitors and doesn't go out much. I never seen you around here before."

"Let's just say I hope we'll become friends," I responded.

He nodded and then thanked me again for coming to his rescue. He unlocked his door, took the bag from me, and entered.

I crossed the hall and knocked on apartment 33C. No music was being played inside today, but I could hear some movement. I waited a moment or two, trying not to be impatient. When she opened the door, Kate Nelson held a damp rag in her hand. She had a scarf on her head, all but hiding her hair, and tied in a knot in the middle above her forehead. The lady was dressed in dark blue pedal pushers—pants ending at midcalf—and a white and blue floral print sleeveless blouse that wasn't tucked in. Surprisingly, she looked very alert, showing no signs of having drunk too much the previous afternoon.

"Hi, remember me?" I asked.

Her face took on a look of irritation.

"Yeah," she said. "You're the guy who wants to give me a message from Abe. Well, turn right around, because I don't want to hear it. He owes me this much. He's not backing out on our arrangement. Go back to your boss and tell him that!"

She started to close the door, but I slipped my foot between it and the jamb, also placing my hand out.

"Hey, wait a minute. Saperstein isn't my boss. I'm not bringing any message from him. I don't even know him."

She became impatient and sighed. "Then who *are* you? What do you want? I ain't done nothin' wrong. I'm playing by all the rules. I'm a good little girl. I don't bother anyone and I don't want anyone bothering me."

"Listen, I'm working on a case. I'm a local PI. I just want to ask you some questions about Abe Saperstein."

"Nuh uh, you ain't connin' me with that one. You just go back to Abe and tell him that his gal Kate is locked at the lips and I'm gonna stay that way."

"If I could just come in and explain—" I began, but she cut me off, shaking her head from side to side.

"No way! This place is torn apart and I'm doin' my cleaning. You ain't comin' in here, Jack."

"Sam," I said.

"What?"

"Sam; the name is Sam." I told her.

"Yeah, well, whatever. *Sam,*" she said with exaggeration. "You ain't comin' in here."

"All right," I said, feeling disappointment. "But I really am a private detective. I was hired by a woman named Sophia Andolucci to look into clearing her husband of a crime he's supposed to have committed. Look me up in the book, that'll prove it. Or better yet, here's one of my cards." I reached into my top shirt pocket, removing one of my business cards, and handed it to her.

She took it and seemed to study it. Without looking up she said, "Andolucci? He's dead, you know."

Kate Nelson had lost the churlishness in her voice. Her frosty manner had been replaced by sadness, and I wondered why. She continued to stare at the card.

"Yes, I know."

"Well, listen…let me mull this over. Why don't you give me some time to think on this? I should have this place back together by late afternoon. Stop back on by after supper tonight." Her eyes rose to mine. "You on the level with this?" she asked.

"Yeah, Kate; I'm on the level."

****

Instead of going in to the office, I made a beeline for Louie's Diner, just a few blocks down the street. I was hungry. When I got there and was seated, I gave a little gal named Doreen my order; three scrambled eggs, hash brown potatoes, pork sausage patties, whole wheat toast, a small tomato juice, and lots of black coffee.

"Go easy on the butter," I told her while handing the menu back to her. This place had a nasty habit of slathering so much butter on toast that it squished when biting into it. After she delivered my coffee, I pulled out a Lucky Strike and lit up, waiting for my food. I felt good; I felt *really* good. Kate Nelson had told me to return to her place this evening. I'd have a chance to talk to her, and even though she might know nothing of Carlo Andolucci or his movements on that day, she might have some information about the hit that Saperstein had ordered. And this afternoon, I would be able to question Mario Nardini. Herschel Sussermann had told me that Nardini was in Saperstein's office the day he was yelling about being ripped off and his wanting the thief to be taken care of. If he was cooperative with me, I might find out exactly what those orders were and who else was in the room. Yep, things were running rather smoothly, I thought.

Soon after I arrived at the diner, people started entering in small groups. I looked at my watch, noting it was eight minutes after 11:00 a.m. It was the beginning of lunch time and workers from area businesses would be piling in, spending their half hour break at the small eatery.

Doreen placed my breakfast in front of me and moved away to coffee a nearby table. I looked at my toast with dismay. Gobs of butter were still melting and running onto the plate. I removed the slices and laid them on a paper napkin on the table, and then I began to eat with gusto. After I was finished there, I wasn't going to go into the office. I'd return to the house on St. Aubin and read the newspaper…I hadn't had a chance to do that this morning. And then, I just might take a short nap before I had to keep that appointment on Adelaide.

CHAPTER NINETEEN

The sun hovered directly above, bouncing heat waves off the hood of the 1938 Chevy as I leaned against it, smoking a cigarette. I was parked directly across from the entrance to the Nardini residence. The same two men I'd run into yesterday when I was there were at their posts up near the porch. They were eying me with curiosity, and I was staring right back. I had no doubt they knew who I was as I noted their smirks. Glancing at my watch, I began to sweat a little at the thought that Augie wouldn't show. It was eight minutes after two o'clock and there had been no sign of him. If he didn't keep our appointment, I was going to look like a fool to these two jerks. I would have no chance at bypassing them to get in to talk to their boss.

I stubbed out my cigarette with the toe of my shoe and eased my hands into my trouser pockets, giving the two across the street a triumphant look. At least I could play with them by making them feel I had the upper hand while I had the chance. A minute later, considerable satisfaction washed over me as I spied Augie's car round the corner. He pulled up and parked directly behind me. Instead of waiting for him to emerge from the vehicle, I started walking toward the gate.

Rico was moving to meet me. He looked back at his buddy when he reached me.

"Hey, looky who's back," he said with a grin on his face.

"I'm here to see Nardini," I said.

"Mickey's right, you don't hear too good."

He unsnapped his shoulder holster, preparing to remove his .22 from it, but that's when Augie came into view, standing beside me. My smile grew wider while Rico's face took on a look of astonishment.

"Hey, Augie," he said. "Long time no see. You know this guy?"

"Yeah," Augie answered. "I want dat we should see Zio Mario."

Ah, I'd forgotten the eloquent way with words this big goon had, and his monotone drove me nuts. I wondered how Gran could stand listening to him talk. Rico gestured in my direction.

"Him, too?"

Augie nodded. On our way up the walk, heading into the house, I leaned just a tad closer to Mickey as we passed him.

"How ya doin' there, big-shot?" I said.

I didn't stop to look at his reaction, but I could well imagine he wasn't happy with my comment.

Augie led me into a vast foyer of elegance. Dark wood paneling covered the lower portion of the wall, and above it, someone had painted a mural of what looked like a quaint Italian village. The colors in the artwork were soft and muted. On our left, we passed an enormous sitting room, sun streaming in through the white lace curtains that hung from gold rods. I briefly spotted a woman sitting on a beige sofa. In the split second I saw her, it registered that she was quite young, with long black hair falling past her shoulders. She was reading a magazine, but looked up as we passed and continued down the hallway. At the end, we made a right turn, entering another hall which had several doors opening onto it. Augie stopped in front of one and looked at me before he entered. I took the hint and waited outside the door. Only moments later, Augie came out to where I stood.

"I'll wait in da parlor," he said, and started retracing his steps to where the young woman was.

"Mr. Nardini?" I said, stepping into the man's bedroom.

This room was twice the size of the living room that Gran and I enjoyed at home. Dark green draperies were pulled back to expose a massive window looking into the rear yard of the property. I could see three large cherry blossom trees and two benches outside. The lawn and bushes were well manicured. It was a nice view. The man sat propped up by numerous pillows on his bed. He wore gray cotton pajamas under a dark blue robe and had brown leather slippers covering his feet. The spread and top sheet were folded neatly down at the foot of where he was laying. Even from his reclining position, I could see he was a tall, gaunt man. Mario Nardini looked all of eighty with his thinning gray hair and moderately wrinkled face. He gestured me to a chair which was placed next to his bed.

"You a friend of my godson?" he asked.

"You could say that. I met him back in January when he was living in Chicago."

He nodded and reached for a glass of water sitting on his bedside table. After taking a sip he said, "So he tells me you're a private gumshoe and you want to speak to me about something. Excuse me for not welcoming you in different surroundings, but I have trouble with my legs. They don't work like they used to. Now, what could you possibly want to find out from me?"

I first told him my name and then recounted how Sophia Andolucci had walked into my office last Saturday to hire me to exonerate her husband in the murders at La Bella Luna.

"That seems like it's going to be difficult, given the amount of years that have passed since then. What luck have you had so far?" he asked.

"Not much pointing me in the right direction to who could have done it, but I'm pretty convinced at this stage that he *didn't* do it."

"Who could you possibly talk to after all these years?"

"I've contacted Kate Nelson. I've yet to really talk to her, but I will. Sophia, herself, told me Carlo was with her at the time of the shootings, and I believe her. And now I'm talking to you," I said. "I hoped you'd be able to tell me who the shooter was; and if not, at least what went on in that office the day Saperstein ordered the hit."

The corners of his lips curved into a small smile. "And who says this hit, as you call it, was ordered by Saperstein?"

"Mr. Nardini, with or without your help, I will find out the truth."

I said nothing more, but kept my eyes even with his. The silence between us didn't last long.

"I sense there is more to this for you. Do you possibly know Carlo's wife on a level deeper than that of client?"

Shaking my head, I said, "I only met the woman on Saturday. But you're right; there's more to it for me. My parents were in that restaurant celebrating their twenty-fifth wedding anniversary. My mother was wounded and my father didn't return to us. So, yes, it's pretty personal. I'm going to find out who murdered my father; and like I said, with or without your help."

"And for that, I am sorry," he said. "Even though my father passed many, many years ago, I know the pain. If Carlo didn't do this, I don't know who did. What else is it that you want to know?"

"First, answer me this…when Andolucci confessed to this crime, were you surprised? Did you believe him?"

The old man shook his head. "No, I did not; or rather, could not. You see, I came over to this fine country as a young man from Reggio di Calabria. It's a small town in the south of Italy. Right across the strait is Sicily. Carlo has Sicilian roots, and I felt as though he was my countryman." He looked at me with a remorseful expression. "That young man was almost like a son to me. I admired him and yes, I loved him, Mr. Flanagan. He was my *paisan*. But there was something more I saw in that young man. I saw a respect…no, a reverence for life. He had high ideals." He shook his head and said in a strengthened voice, "No, he didn't belong with the gang. I knew that and Abe knew it. And Abe only tolerated him out of respect for me. Don't get me wrong; we could depend on Carlo for collections and such. But Abe didn't use him for much more, and he knew how I felt about the boy."

"So, if the two of you knew that Carlo wasn't the type to carry out such a crime, why order him to do it?"

Nardini looked at me, surprised. "Carlo wasn't ordered to do it. Abe would never have trusted him to do such a thing. Had he ordered the boy to carry out a hit, he knew Carlo would've refused and he'd have to take disciplinary measures. And then, had that happened, I would not have been happy."

This was a bit of surprising news to me. If Andolucci wasn't given the job of whacking the driver who was stealing some of the shipments of liquor, who had been?

"Who did Saperstein give this job to, then?"

"The Kid, Billy Levinthal. Anytime Saperstein had to eliminate a problem, he usually called on Levinthal. Eh, the guy delighted in such assignments. He was one sick bastard. And to tell you how sick he was, he'd been friends with this driver. Brought him into the fold because this guy needed extra money. Had a huge family to support, as I recall. So, the man works his day job, and by night, he makes pick ups and deliveries. Only he got a bit too greedy as time went on. Abe had suspected, but wasn't sure. He calls someone in and they rat on the guy. So, this gent becomes expendable. And Levinthal doesn't care one damn bit that he has to pop his friend."

Movement caught my eye and I looked slightly to my right. Nardini followed my gaze. The woman who had been reading a magazine when I'd first entered with Augie was standing in the doorway. Seeing her closely for the first time, I could see she was older than I'd originally thought. She could have been anywhere between thirty and thirty-five years of age.

"What is it, Teresa?" Nardini asked.

In a whiny voice, she responded, "I want to *do* something, Mario. We sit in this house like we're prisoners. I want to go out tonight. Let's do something different. And now I have that goofball sitting across from me, and all he does is stare while I'm trying to read my magazine. He gives me the creeps."

Nardini's face reddened and his lips grew taut.

"Whatsa matter with you? Can't you see I'm talking to this gentleman? And who are you to call my godson such names? Get outta here!"

"Come on, Mario," she persisted. "Let's do something! Let's go out for the evening tonight."

"And do what? You want me to take you dancing?" he asked sarcastically. "Oh yes, Teresa, hand me my cane and we'll go. Now get outta here! Tell Mickey to take you uptown and go buy yourself a new dress or a pair of earrings or something."

She kept pushing her luck and stamped her foot on the floor.

"What for, Mario? Where would I ever wear it?" she spouted.

I was surprised by the swiftness with which he reacted, suddenly reaching down to remove a slipper. He hurled the shoe across the room, aiming it at her. She moved just in time and it hit the wall behind her. At that, she decided to disappear from sight.

"Now stay outta here till my business is finished!" he yelled. And then turning back to me, he said, "Eh, the dizzy dame! I shoulda lived out the rest of my life alone when my first wife died, God rest her soul."

This little break in our conversation wasn't going to deter me. I was eager for him to continue.

"Mr. Nardini, can you just tell me what went on in Saperstein's office that day? Who was there? Why was Carlo Andolucci there if this assignment wasn't being given to him?"

He shrugged. "I can't recall the reason he was there. Maybe Abe had a collection for him to run. But before the fellas arrived, Abe had been in a state after learning for sure this guy was skimming off the top of the product. He was hot under the collar and nothing would settle him down. So he calls in Billy Levinthal and a guy named Haim Ehrenfeld. Haimie is to take the guy to the restaurant, sit in the corner booth by the door, and at a few minutes to six, he's to excuse himself and go to the john. Levinthal enters, pops him, job done. That's the way it was supposed to go down. No one else gets hurt. But that isn't what happened. Not only does this guy eat lead, but so does Haimie, along with a lot of others."

"Levinthal arrives early?" I asked.

"Levinthal says he never got there. He claims he's approaching the restaurant in his auto and sees people crowding the front of the building and three cop cars pull up. So he keeps on going."

"But if he's lying, and he did get there early…well, do you think Andolucci would protect him by saying it was he, himself, who did this?"

Nardini was shaking his head.

"Who knows? All I know is that I went down to that jail to talk to Carlo and he refused to see me. If he was that close to the Kid, I sure wasn't aware of it."

I stared at the old man for a moment, feeling puzzled.

"Why do you tell me all of this?"

"Look at me. I'm an old man, Flanagan. What do I care? Let's just say I might want to honor Carlo in death. And, of course, out of respect for your father."

"Where is Billy Levinthal now? Is he still in town?"

"Your guess would be as good as mine. He left town years ago, but who knows if he's returned?"

I reached for one of my business cards and handed it to him, asking him to call me if he thought of anything else. It was time to go. I felt I'd learned everything I could from the man. Before reaching the door, Nardini called me back.

"I just did you a big favor, Flanagan. Now you do me one."

I waited for him to tell me just what that favor might be.

"Let me know if you find out that someone else did this. Let me know who it was. Let's just say I'd like to speak to him."

I took my leave without another word.

CHAPTER TWENTY

It was just past three thirty when I pulled up in the driveway on St. Aubin. I found Gran on her knees, pulling weeds in between the bushes that lined the front porch. Young Bobby Randle from next door was helping her. His brother, Albie, wasn't in sight. She looked up when I got out of the Chevy.

"Sam, do you have some money?" She turned and caressed the back of the boy's head. "I needed someone to help me with these weeds."

Well, why not? Feeling particularly generous since I'd only be paying out to one boy, I offered the young lad fifty cents if he could finish up by himself. Gran's face, neck, and upper chest were flushed and I could see sweat rolling down the sides of her cheeks from her temples. He agreed. I climbed the porch steps behind my grandmother, but before we could enter, Albie came around the side of the house from the backyard.

"Mrs. Flanagan, you want me to pull the weeds along the fence in the very back, too?"

Aw, hell; now I was going to be out a dollar!

****

We ate an early dinner and then listened to the Tiger game on the wireless. It was a good game; Dizzy Trout pitched all nine innings, and the Tigers beat the Philadelphia Athletics at home by a score of 3-0. As we listened, Gran sipped on a cold beer while I had to keep my mind from wandering. Honestly, I didn't think there was much point in making the trip out to Kate Nelson's in light of what Mario Nardini had told me. I mean, what could she add to what he'd already said? But on the off chance she could tell me anything at all about Billy Levinthal, I'd keep our appointment. Besides, I was curious about something–who the hell was Sid Buczynski?

At ten minutes to seven o'clock, I scooped up my keys off the kitchen counter. The phone rang before I could make my exit.

"Hello?"

"Flanagan?"

The voice was deep and raspy, belonging to a man. I squinted, trying to figure out who was calling me.

"Speaking," I said.

"You workin' on the Andolucci case?"

"Yes," I said immediately.

For some reason, I thought this guy might have some information for me, and I jumped at it without thinking.

"Well, lay off, you hear? Drop it before you get yourself in hot water."

"Who *is* this?"

"You heard me. You just quit nosin' around and you won't get hurt. You been warned."

"Now just a minute," I said with indignation, and then I heard a click on the other end. He'd hung up.

****

Kate Nelson was still dressed in her peddle pushers and blouse, but her hair was free of the scarf. Her black bangs covered her forehead and she wore pink lipstick.

"I thought you might have changed your mind," she said as she ushered me into the apartment.

I followed her through approximately six feet of narrow hallway, which opened onto a spacious and well decorated living area. The room contained two small dark blue sofas, sitting perpendicular to each other, with an oval, maple wood coffee table placed in front of them. The furniture pieces sat on a large floral area rug which contained blue, green and burgundy. A Philco combination radio and record player stood against the wall opposite one of the sofas, positioned under a large oval, gold framed mirror. Two matching floor lamps were in the room, as was a small table near the opening to the compact kitchen, just large enough to hold her telephone. The place not only looked attractive, but also smelled clean and fresh with the scent of lavender polish. Removing my hat, I took a seat on one of the sofas.

"Would you like a drink? I have some bourbon and a bit of gin," she offered.

"Are you going to have one?"

She laughed with embarrassment. "After yesterday, I don't think so. I'm going to put a pot of coffee on for myself."

"Coffee sounds good to me, also," I said. "If you don't mind, that is."

"Not at all. I don't have any cream, though."

"I drink it black," I told her.

She moved away from me, entering the next room. I saw only one other door leading to another room, and I suspected it was her bedroom. The bathroom, I assumed, had to be off of it. I was quite impressed.

"So, how is Abe doing these days?" she called out.

I chuckled. "I told you, I don't know him. I'm working for Sophia Anders, wife of Carlo Andolucci."

She appeared in the doorway, facing me, a glass canister of coffee and a scoop in her hand.

"Anders?"

"After he went to prison, she changed her name to Anders, but now she wants the name of Andolucci back."

"Why?" she asked.

"She's got a son who's getting interested in a young lady. She wants him to return to his rightful name. That's what she says, anyway." I shrugged.

She went back to making the coffee and I waited for her patiently. She took a seat on the other sofa when she reentered the living room. Popping sounds of the percolator reached my ears.

"So," she said. "Why are you interested in Abe?"

"I'm not really. I'm more interested in a contract he put out years ago. I want to know who actually carried it out. Carlo Andolucci took the rap for it, but I don't think he did it. Neither does his wife. She wants me to prove it, and she feels that she can then return to her married name; her and her son." I hesitated and then said, "But before we get into that, can I ask you a personal question?"

"Go ahead," she replied. "But I'm making no promises that I'll answer it."

"Who is Sid Buczynski, and why did you think he might be dead?"

Kate Nelson threw her head back and loud laughter emerged from her. It was contagious and I began to laugh aloud also, although I didn't know why the question struck her as being so funny. The palm of her hand came down and slapped the cushion of the couch beside her leg.

"Ah," she said, attempting to compose herself. "When you first came to the door, I thought you might be his attorney and I thought I was in for a big windfall." She took in the confused look on my face. "Once upon a time, Mr. Flanagan, he was my husband. You see, I had a mother who was a tyrant and a daddy who I just adored, but who died when I was twelve. Left to live with her alone was unbearable. I don't know how he stood it, himself. At sixteen, I was outta there…no looking back. Just took off one night with nothing but the clothes on my back and three dollars and forty-five cents that I was able to pinch from her purse. I went to the bus station and couldn't quite decide where I wanted to go, so I ended up sleeping in the terminal for two nights before a Mr. Sid Buczynski came along. He asked me about myself, asked me if I was hungry. I jumped at the chance to get a square meal. The man fed me and then offered to take me home to stay with him and his mother until I could figure out my next move."

She glanced at me and noted the interested look on my face. She continued.

"I should have been leery. It's not good to just go off with a stranger, no matter who he presents himself as, but I wasn't. I was cold and tired and I didn't want to worry about where my next meal came from. Anyway, to make a long story short, I ended up marrying him when he suggested it. He said he could take care of me. He had his own watch repair shop in the city and Mama had money; lots of it. We lived with his mother the whole time. I was sixteen and he was thirty-five. I'd never been so bored and felt so trapped in all my life. I didn't love him in the least, but Sid was good to me. He was kind, but he wanted a little girl to raise. He didn't want a wife, and I didn't want an old man. I don't say that so much because of his age. He was actually an old man in spirit, and yet, he was a little boy when it came to his mother. *She* was the real woman in his life." She shrugged. "So, I left him, but he told me I would always be welcomed back and that he would provide for me in his will. I haven't seen him in years."

"Where'd you go from there?" I asked.

"Eh, he gave me some money. I ended up at a boarding house on the east side. I was trying to find a job during the day, and went past a small night club advertising for a singer. Daddy used to say I sounded like an angel, and I loved to sing; so I went in and applied. The place was a dive, really, but I got the job. And *that* is where I met Abe Saperstein. I met him in 1921 and I was twenty-three at the time. God," she said. "That's ages ago." She looked at me with her dark brown eyes boring into mine and asked, "So, what's your story? You married?"

I shook my head and gave a short laugh. "Not anymore. She left me years ago. She had other plans; she had dreams that didn't include me."

"Ah, that's a shame. Good lookin' guy like you? I figured you'd be married and have a dozen kids."

"Nope," I said. "So, it got serious with Saperstein?"

"Yes and no," she said. "He set me up in this place and bought me the best in furs and jewelry—and yes, we were lovers. But it didn't take me long to figure out I didn't love him. He wasn't a nice guy, you know? Oh, don't get me wrong, he wasn't violent with me, but he could be ruthless if he didn't like you or you'd crossed him in some way. But by the time I knew I didn't really love him, I'd gotten too used to what he could give me. And I was a good listener. I think he kept me around for that. Some of his boys would come round, too."

"How about Levinthal? Would he come around?"

She nodded her head. "Yeah, a couple of times, until I complained to Abe about him."

She suddenly rose from her sitting position and entered the kitchen, bringing with her two cups of black coffee when she returned.

"What were the complaints?" I asked when she sat back down on the sofa.

"He was a little too free with his hands," she said. "He thought he could take liberties, and he couldn't. Abe's men sometimes came to visit or just talk, and that's all it was. Even if Abe didn't care, I did. I wasn't having any of that, if you know what I mean." She looked around the room and sighed, waving her hand. "So this is it. I'm left with this place, which Abe still pays for, and a small allowance he sends. I've sold all the jewelry and furs; hocked them all. I needed the money they could bring in." Her hand rose to touch the pearl earring clipped on her right lobe. "This is it. It's all I have left; this one pair of earrings. I don't own one other single piece of jewelry, but I don't care. Abe set me up in the best places to sing and I made a lot of money doing it, but it's all gone now."

"Why aren't you still singing?" I asked her.

"Look at me, Mr. Flanagan. I'm forty-five years old and my figure isn't what it used to be. The voice is still strong, but who would hire me now? Nope, this is it. I pretty much live my life within these four walls. I've only been in love once in my life, but that wasn't to be. I spend time in here reliving the past and dreaming of what could've been."

"If not Sid Buczynski or Abe Saperstein, then who?" I found myself asking, and then quickly said, "Sorry, I don't mean to pry."

Kate Nelson hesitated, gazing into my eyes. She was struggling with whether to reveal the man she'd been in love with. She inhaled deeply.

"Oh hell, why not?" she said. "It was Carlo...Carlo Andolucci. I fell in love with that man very soon after I met him."

"Did he know?" I asked her.

"Nah," she shook her head. "I never told him. He was deeply in love with his wife. She was his whole world."

****

By the time I left the Somerset Apartments, dark clouds had rolled into the city, threatening a downpour. I'd spent three hours in the company of Kate Nelson, listening to her reminisce and answer my questions concerning the shooting nineteen years ago and her thoughts about Andolucci's confession. And surprisingly, I spent much of the time talking about myself, finding it quite easy to reveal certain things to this woman. I could see why members of the gang wanted to be in her presence. Carlo Andolucci was no exception. She told me that he would come to just talk and she would listen to how it bothered him to carry out some of the orders that his boss, Saperstein, had given him. He'd told her of how he was making plans to open a small business of his own, and of his desire to leave the gang and its activities behind. The man was even more determined to abandon his life of crime since he'd been told of his wife's pregnancy. Kate said he'd been appreciative of Abe Saperstein's generosity in giving him a place within the organization, but he just couldn't do it anymore. He knew the time had come to move on. She also told me she'd worried about this, feeling Carlo was being naïve about how things worked. She wondered if the handsome Sicilian knew it might be more difficult to distance himself from the Purples and Saperstein than he was aware.

In the end, I found that she, too, didn't believe he'd gone into La Bella Luna and committed the crime he'd confessed to. She had wanted to go to the jail to beg him not to go through with this confession, or to at least accept council, but she didn't dare. How would she explain her interest to Saperstein? Kate Nelson couldn't risk losing her meal ticket.

At hearing this, I now had my doubts that the young enforcer would've taken the fall at the orders of the leader of the Purple Gang...why would he when he wanted out? So who would motivate him to take the rap? Someone he was protecting? Levinthal? Someone else I'd yet to hear about? Kate didn't know who he was that close to in the organization, so she couldn't point me in the right direction. When asked if she knew if Levinthal was still in the city, she said she didn't know and didn't care, calling him "nothing but a little puke." I'd have to talk to Sophia and see if her husband had ever mentioned someone he viewed as a special friend.

I kept replaying my visit with Kate Nelson over and over in my mind while I lay in the dark on the couch in the parlor.

"Did Sophia ever know of his visits to you?" I'd asked Miss Nelson.

She shook her head, "Nah, I don't believe so. I don't think he even thought of me outside of this apartment," she'd answered.

It had to be approaching midnight, and I'd yet to fall asleep. Deep, rumbling thunder sounded outside and a wonderful breeze entered the front room, a breeze that wasn't flowing through the window in my bedroom. Just before dozing off, I thought of how I'd made my way down to the Chevy from the woman's apartment that night, not realizing that I'd worn a giddy smile all the way on route. Kate was that easy to be with. My very last thought before unconsciousness overtook me was about the phone call I'd received. Who in the hell could that have been?

Just how long I'd been asleep when I heard the noise, I didn't know. Someone had bumped into the coffee table which was in front of the sofa where I'd been lying. Gran? I could see her silhouette in the dimness of the room, only it didn't really look like her. Rain was hitting the rooftop with steady splats. I wondered what she was doing and why she was out of bed. Rising on one elbow, I called out to her.

"Gran?"

In an instant the breath was knocked out of me by the form pouncing on me, landing on my chest and knocking me back again. A fear shot through me as I realized the intruder was a man and my grandmother was behind her bedroom door and in danger as well. I tried to fight back, but my arms were pinned to my sides by the man's knees. He roughly took my jaw in his hand, clamping my mouth shut.

"I told you to lay off, Flanagan!" he growled with clenched teeth.

I tried to wiggle my head free of his grasp, but he was too strong. In the almost pitch black, I could make out that his right hand rose in the air and formed a fist. Down it came into my face; not once, not twice, but three times. He made contact in the same spot all three times…my left cheekbone. It felt shattered under a pair of brass knuckles. He may have hit me several times more, but after the third punch, my world went black.

CHAPTER TWENTY-ONE

I woke Friday morning to the sting of mercurochrome being applied to my face by Gran. Recoiling from the pain, I struggled to move away from her.

"Now stay still!" she scolded me. "Goodness sake, what in the world did you run into last night, dear?"

"It wasn't what *I* ran into; it's what ran into me. Someone was in here last night and my face met his fist. I think he was wearing brass knuckles."

"In *here* last night? I didn't hear a thing."

"No, I guess you wouldn't have with that fan running in your room," I told her. "How bad is it? At the time, it felt like he shattered my cheekbone. Is my eye swollen? It feels swollen."

"Yes, it's swollen and it's the prettiest shade of purple." I tried to roll my eyes, but it hurt too much. "I don't think any bones are shattered, though," she said. "Here, does this hurt?"

She took the tips of her fingers and pressed into my cheekbone.

"*Ouch*!" I screamed. "*What are you trying to do*?"

"Well, it feels like your bone is in one piece, dear."

She screwed the cap back on the little brown bottle of orange colored medicine and rose from the edge of the sofa, allowing me to move to a sitting position.

"Maybe you should see a doctor, dear," she suggested.

"No, I'll be all right."

As she walked toward the back of the house, she called over her shoulder, "Well, you look like you could play a part in one of those horror movies, dear."

"Gee, thanks a lot," I said, but the mere act of speaking made me wince with pain.

****

Even the spray of the tepid shower water caused me discomfort when it hit my battered cheek. Lathering the cloth, I barely applied any pressure while washing my face. Who had done this to me? I could figure out the "why." Someone was very anxious for me to stop this investigation. Someone out there had been carrying around a damaging secret for over nineteen years. I had to find out who that someone was, and then I was quite sure I'd have the person who'd murdered my father and who'd maimed my mother. But, in the meantime, what was I going to do about my grandmother? Surely, she could be in danger if this someone decided to return.

Emerging from the bathroom in my robe, I heard voices coming from just beyond the side kitchen window where Shamus was perched on the sill. I moved closer and bent to see who it was. Gran was talking with Mae Randle, the mother of Albie and Bobby, over the chain link fence. Now was my chance! I moved to the telephone on the wall near the back door and dialed Helen Foster's number. After identifying myself when she answered, I told her I needed her to do a huge favor for me. She was silent.

"Oh come on, Helen. This is important. I need to bring Gran over there. Let her stay for a few days. Someone broke in here last night and I'm afraid for her safety if he comes back."

"Broke in?" she asked with astonishment. "Did they steal anything? Is she all right?"

"She's just fine; it was me he was after. Nothing was stolen. He came here to leave me a message and he delivered it," I explained.

"Huh?"

"Never mind," I said. "Can I count on you?"

"Well, certainly," she said, as though I were an imbecile for thinking she *wouldn't* help out. "But I'm just getting ready to walk out. My nephew is coming over to pick me up. I'll be visiting with him and his wife for a few hours today. Bring her by later this afternoon."

"Oh, and Helen, let her think this was *your* idea…that you invited her."

After disconnecting, I dialed the home number of Sophia Anders, asking for her when her brother, Nito, answered. I wanted to swing by her apartment and bring her up to speed on the investigation.

"She ain't home. She's at work, but she'll be here after one o'clock. She'll have the rest of the day off; you can come by then."

Since I couldn't see Sophia Anders until that afternoon, I figured I'd make an appearance at the office, but I was in no hurry. I went in search of the newspaper, and after finding it on the end table in the living room, I brought it back with me to the kitchen and proceeded to fix myself a bowl of cereal.

****

The rain had stopped, leaving the air fresh and clean. The sky was returning to its light blue hue, and a wonderful breeze entered the windows of my Woodward Avenue second story office. I twirled a pencil as Frankie Kirkendahl sat across from me at my desk.

"You say you don't know if this Billy Levinthal is in the city?" she asked.

"That's right. Someone said he left town years ago, but I don't know when, and I don't know if he ever came back."

She reached over and grabbed another pencil and a scrap sheet of paper.

"Let me see what I can do," she said. "Bil-ly Le-vin-thal. There; did I spell it right?" she asked, showing me what she'd written on the paper.

"Yep, that's it, all right."

The young woman rose from her chair and headed for the door. I stopped her with a question.

"Hey," I said. "Why you being so nice to me? What gives?"

She pointed her forefinger in my direction.

"Have you taken a look in the mirror? You're wearing more colors on your face than the rainbow has. Can you even see out of that one eye?"

"Barely," I responded.

"Well, that's why. I feel sorry for you, Mr. Flanagan."

I smiled and then winced, the palm of my hand flying to the left side of my face; but by then, she'd already walked across the hall.

****

Someone was entering the Harrington Arms just as I reached the steps. I quickened my pace and followed them in, and therefore bypassed using the buzzer to announce my presence. When I reached Sophia's door, I gave a short knock, and it was almost immediately answered by Nito. His smile turned into a frown when he laid eyes on me. He whistled softly.

"Holy Moly," he said. "What happened to you?"

"I ran into a fist," I explained.

"Must've been one helluva big fist," he remarked. "Either that or you ran into it quite a few times."

"Yeah, something like that."

"Well, come on in. Sophia ain't here yet, but she should be anytime now."

He held the door open wide enough for me to enter and move past him. I headed straight for the chair that I'd sat in a couple of days ago. I removed my hat, setting it on the arm of the chair, and glanced at my watch. It was thirteen minutes after one o'clock.

"Don't worry, she'll be here. She don't go nowhere but to work and the market once in a while."

He sat on the sofa across from me, which made me a bit uncomfortable, given how our first meeting had gone. He must have sensed my uneasiness.

"Listen, I suppose we got off on the wrong foot. I'm sorry for bein' so rude the other day, but it's just that I don't wanna see Sophia get hurt. She's worked hard her whole life for what she has, and I don't wanna see her waste it on somethin' that might not pan out, ya know?"

I nodded.

"I mean, if you can finger whoever did this, then by all means, it's a good thing she hired you. But if you can't, well...," he shrugged. "She forgets I loved Carlo, too. He was the only one who took an interest in me outside of my sister back then. He was like a second father to me. It's just that I don't see how this thing can be solved after all this time."

"Listen, Nito; I'm not going to take your sister for a ride. If I find I'm not getting anywhere, I'll let her know. I'll reimburse her any money I haven't earned. Fair enough?"

"Yeah," he said while nodding. "Hey, you want somethin' to drink? She ain't got no beer or nothin' like that."

"A glass of water would be nice."

Nito rose and made his way to the kitchen, and my eyes settled on the pictures of Carlo Andolucci and his son again. I wondered if young Carlo lived here; I hadn't seen him either time I'd been in this apartment. Did he attend school? I couldn't remember if Sophia had told me that or not. Father and son looked so much alike. This young fellow and I had something in common. We'd both lost our fathers way too prematurely. Was his father as important to him as mine was to me? Did he even really know the senior Carlo very well?

Nito was making his way back to me when I heard the door open. Sophia entered, but she stopped when she saw me.

"Oh, Mr. Flanagan," she said, surprised. "Do you have news for me?" She was staring at my face. "My goodness, what happened?"

"You've just come in; why don't you do whatever it is you do to get comfortable after work? Get yourself some tea or whatever and then come to sit down. I want to tell you what I've found out so far."

She moved to the sofa, setting her purse down on the coffee table, and I took a sip of my water.

"No, I'd like to hear what you have to say," she said, nervously.

"First of all, I don't believe your husband walked into that restaurant and killed anyone," I said. "I've spoken with some who knew him and they don't believe it either."

Sophia turned to her brother who sat next to her and placed her hand on his arm.

"You see, Nito; I knew he was innocent!" she said with excitement in her voice and on her face. She then turned back to me. "All those times when I first went to the prison, I begged him to tell me the truth, and all he would say was 'Leave it alone, Sophia. I did it.' But I *knew* he was lying for some reason. So, who have you talked to?"

"A man who was in the organization your husband worked for named Mario Nardini. Do you know him?"

"I only saw him a couple of times, but I remember him. Who else?"

"I made a trip out to the man who was assigned to defend him from the public defenders office. He thought your husband's confession was a bit fishy, too. I talked to a man who was in the restaurant that evening. He described as best he could the shooter, and it just doesn't seem like his description fit Carlo."

"Why not?" Nito asked.

"He says the shooter came in wearing denim pants and sneakers. From everyone I've spoken with, Carlo was a snazzy dresser. It just doesn't go with everything I've heard about him."

Sophia started to laugh and touched her brother's arm again.

"That's true, isn't it, Nito? Carlo always had to look so dapper wherever he went. It was so important to him. And, Mr. Flanagan; he didn't even own a pair of sneakers. I know that for a fact!"

"Yeah, he was a real pip, all right; always togged to the bricks," Nito said.

"The thing is," I resumed. "That's the easy part…coming to the conclusion that your husband actually didn't commit this crime. It's going to be harder finding out who did. I figure he must have been protecting someone; either that, or he was ordered to take the fall for the job, but I don't think so. The protection angle seems more likely to me. Is there anyone he was really close to in the gang?"

Sophia shook her head. "I don't think so."

"Now think, Sophia. Is there anyone he used to talk about more than anyone else? Did he ever mention a Billy Levinthal?"

She shook her head again. "I don't think so. If he did, I don't remember. I don't recognize that name, but he did speak of Mr. Nardini. Carlo liked the man and respected him. I think he told me once that Mr. Nardini was real good to him, just like an uncle or a father. That's all I know. He rarely, if ever, spoke about what he did or the people he worked with."

"I'll give this more time," I said. "I had a call yesterday from someone warning me to stay away from this investigation. Although I'm not sure, I believe it was the same guy who broke into my home last night and decided to deliver his message in a different way…with his fist. I'm making someone out there pretty nervous, and that's a good sign."

"Oh my goodness," Sophia uttered. "Please be careful, Mr. Flanagan." She rose from the sofa. "I'm going to pay you for another couple of days. I really appreciate all you've done so far."

When she stood, Nito grabbed the Saturday Evening Post from the table in front of him, and was now lying on the sofa, his face behind it. She started to move farther into the apartment when the phone rang, and I heard her answer it. A moment later, she stood at my side, telling me the caller had asked for me. Who would be calling me there? Frankie knew I was coming to see Sophia, but I didn't leave her the number. I doubted she would have much trouble in getting it, though. She seemed to have a knack for finding things out. And then a sudden thought struck me—*Gran*! I told her I was coming here this afternoon and showed her the number I'd tacked up near our telephone, just in case she needed me for anything. The fear of the mystery goon paying another visit shot through me. I hurried to answer the call, while Sophia entered her bedroom.

"Hi, Sam."

The voice on the other end wasn't my grandmother and it wasn't Frankie, but it was definitely female. I thought I recognized it.

"Miss Nelson? How did you know where I would be?"

"Because I called your house and a woman told me you were there. I thought you said you weren't married. Tell me that was your maid," she said.

I laughed into the receiver. "Something like that. That was my grandmother."

"You live with your grandmother?" she asked.

"I sure do. Now what can I do for you, Miss Nelson?"

"Hey, you mean to tell me after last night we're back to Miss Nelson? The name is Kate, Sam."

"Okay, Kate then."

"Well, listen…I got to thinking about what you were trying to find out. Who would Carlo try to protect? The only one I can think of would be the kid. It has to be him. I think his name was Buddy, or maybe Benny or Billy; something like that. I'm not sure, but it all makes sense to me."

"Okay," I said, trying to follow her.

The kid. Who mentioned that phrase when talking to me? It was Nardini. Nardini had referred to Levinthal as the Kid, hadn't he? And hadn't we just talked about Levinthal last night? Did we mention his first name of Billy? Didn't she know that was his name? I was a bit confused.

"The kid? Could the kid possibly be Levinthal?"

"I'm not going to say another word until tonight," she said. "I have this fabulous idea and I'm wondering if you'll go along with it."

"Okay, let's hear your idea."

She hesitated and I looked from where I stood back into the living room. Nito was lying in the same position, but his face was now covered with the magazine. He'd fallen asleep.

"Well, I hope you don't think I'm being too forward, but what are you doing tonight?"

"I don't know, why?" I asked.

"Well, gee, Sam. Don't you ever get lonely? I mean, all I do is sit here and no one ever comes to visit."

"So you want me to come visit tonight," I laughed.

"No," she said with enthusiasm. "I want to go out on the town; how about it? You could do worse, ya know? And besides, I'm not *that* much older than you."

She didn't say another word, but I could feel her nervousness through the telephone wire.

"Kate Nelson," I teased, while wearing a broad smile. "Are you asking me out on a date?"

Her voice cracked. "I guess you could call it that, but I understand if you have other plans."

"I don't, and you're right. I could do a helluva lot worse…but maybe you can't."

"What do you mean?" she asked.

"My face is a bit messed up. I've got some swelling and a lot of pretty colors to go with it. In fact, my grandmother told me I could be a candidate for starring in a horror film. You sure you want to be seen with me?"

"Oh, never mind, I'll know what you're talking about when you get here."

I glanced at my watch. It was twenty minutes after two. "How about I pick you up in a couple of hours? We'll get a bite to eat and then go to the Grande Ballroom for a night of dancing."

"Don't you dare!" she said with excitement in her voice. "I gotta get ready, and boy do I have an evening gown to make your eyes pop out! I'm gonna be dressed to the hilt this evening, Mr. Flanagan! Pick me up at six thirty. We'll get a bite to eat and then let's go to the Vanity Ballroom instead. I haven't been there in ages."

"I'll see you at six thirty then."

After disconnecting, Sophia handed me a ten dollar bill and two fives. She walked me to the door, where we passed Nito, who was starting to snore. As I made my way down to the Chevy, which was parked across the street, I was wearing that giddy grin again...which made my cheek hurt like hell. I tried to wipe it off my face, but was unsuccessful.

CHAPTER TWENTY-TWO

It was a quarter of four when I pulled into Helen Foster's driveway with Gran at my side. My grandmother's friend had come through like a trooper…not only was she going to play this off like it was her idea, but she'd called Gran in my absence to apologize and beg her to come back and spend a few nights. They could have one long sleeping over party, she'd told her. She had planned a night for the two of them playing Old Maid while listening to the new radio production of "My Sister Eileen" on Lux Radio Theater.

Gran got out of the Chevy holding her overnight bag and her six pack of Champagne Velvet beer. I hadn't seen her this thrilled in days. Helen came out of her front door, putting an arm around her friend, Ruby Flanagan, and led her inside the house. They'd forgotten about me, leaving me standing at the base of the porch steps. I climbed them and knocked on the screen door. When Helen glanced back, I waved her over.

"What?" she asked harshly.

I leaned in closer to the screen, saying, "If this door wasn't between us, I'd take you in my arms and kiss you!"

Her eyes widened and she leaned back. "Oh go on, you fool!" And then she squinted with her eyes, seeming to notice my injury for the first time. "You look like hell," she said.

I laughed, making my way back to the running automobile.

****

Honest to God, I felt like a school boy. You'd think this was the first time I was going to take a woman out on a proper date. I believe I felt a fluttering in my gut. Butterflies? But the bare truth was, I enjoyed being with Kate Nelson. Somehow, I felt a comfort with her that had been missing with the young boutique owner, Patti Ann. I somehow felt as though I'd known the former singer for years, and that she was my close friend. I didn't know where this would lead, but I wanted it to become that, at least—a close friendship. Only time would tell.

It was just going on four thirty, so instead of taking a quick shower, I opted for a lingering warm bath. I was eager to learn what Kate's theory was in this case. What information did she have for me? But I was also eager to just enjoy myself; to get away from the case, too, and have a few laughs with her. An intermission would serve me well; it always did. When trying to crack a case, I found that I periodically needed a break from it in order to see things clearly.

At five twenty-five, I was out of the tub, clean-shaven, and dressed in my best suit; the navy blue one. For some inexplicable reason, I wanted to hear Kate's voice…I couldn't explain the sudden urgency. I picked up the telephone receiver and dialed her number, trying to think of a reason for the call.

"Hi," I said when she answered. "What color is your gown?"

"Why?" she laughed.

"Because I'm not sure what suit to wear."

"Tell me about the suits."

"I've got my everyday brown suit. I've got a sharp looking black suit with a rip in the seam of the trousers. And I've got my newer dark blue suit."

She laughed again, a more hearty laugh.

"Uh, gee, that's a tough decision. Hey, I've got a suggestion...why don't you wear the dark blue suit?"

"Good idea," I said. "See you in about an hour."

The next forty-five minutes passed in slow motion. I fed the kitten and then paced the floor; then I paced the floor some more. Just as I was reaching for my keys, a knock came on the front door. Standing by my dresser in the bedroom, I hesitated. What if it was my attacker, returning to see if I'd heeded his message? But then I chuckled inside—he'd hardly knock, now would he? Along with the keys, I scooped up my bills and slipped them into my pants pocket.

Albie Randle was standing on the front porch, his brother Bobby out on the walk. When I opened the screen a few inches, he looked at me from head to toe.

"Whoa, you look purdy keen, Mr. Flanagan. Where ya goin'? You smell good, too."

"Thanks," I said. "I took a bath."

He laughed. "Well, where ya goin'?"

"On a date," I replied.

"With who?"

"You don't know her."

"You goin' out to dinner with her?"

"I might," I answered.

"You gonna marry her?"

"I might."

"Wow," he exclaimed. "Wouldn't that be kippy?"

"It might be. Hey, what is this, twenty questions?"

He laughed again. "Nah, Ma said we could walk up to the Stop and Shop, but we don't have any money. We thought you could pay us what you owe us for pullin' those weeds."

"I owe you money?" I said, teasing the boy.

He said nothing, but just stood there and stared at me. I began to laugh.

"Okay, I guess I can part with it."

I reached into my pocket, drawing out my bills and some change. Handing him a dollar bill, I also thumbed through my coins and gave him two nickels. Yes, I know…I usually complained about parting with my hard-earned dough, but I was feeling especially upbeat at the moment.

He smiled. "Hey, gee, thanks!"

Before he could descend the porch, I said, "Hang on." I backed away from the door and picked up the comic book the kids had given me for my birthday. It had been sitting on the end table. "Here, I read this. Can you keep it for me for a while?"

His smile grew wider. "Sure!"

****

The evening was mild, the temperature being no more than seventy-five degrees. A pleasant and steady wind blew through the streets of Detroit. As I made my way to the Somerset Apartments, "All of Me," a tune from ten years ago or more, was filling the inside of the Chevy. I sang right along with Mildred Bailey.

All of me, why not take all of me?
Can't you see, I'm no good without you?
Take my lips; I want to lose them.
Take my arms; I never use them….

Pulling up to the building, I noticed the same kids playing marbles I'd seen on another visit. I parked in front, and then sidestepped them as I approached the door. Taking the stairs two at a time, I was eager to see Kate in her gown, whatever color it was. As I neared her apartment, I could hear no music or any other sound coming from within. I knocked. Under my touch, her door moved inward a couple of inches. I smiled, knowing she'd left it unlatched for me to enter when I arrived. Stepping just inside, I called out her name. When she didn't answer, I moved farther into the apartment, shutting the door behind me.

"Kate?" I called out again. "I'm here and my feet are itching to slide across that dance floor."

I was standing just before the entrance to the living room, not wanting to step in the apartment all the way just in case I'd catch her off guard and not fully dressed. But from my vantage point, I could see that her bedroom door was opened and there was a beautiful silk jade green gown lying across her bed. And then something caught my eye and I looked down at the floor. There I saw the perfectly painted red toe nails of Kate Nelson.

CHAPTER TWENTY-THREE

I could see her feet, but she wasn't standing. Quickly, I went to where she was laying. Kate Nelson was lying on her back in the doorway, her upper body in the kitchen, while below her waist rested in her living room. She was wearing a white terry cloth robe, the belt of it wrapped around her neck. There was ugly bruising underneath that belt. Her eyes were partly opened; the fine, spidery vessels had burst in the whites of them. The same with her face—blood vessels had broken across her cheeks, on her forehead and chin. Kneeling beside her, I placed the tips of my fingers at her throat. *Dear God, no! Be alive! Breathe! Come on, Kate! Damn it, breathe!* I had no idea if I was saying it aloud, but it was too late…she was gone.

In the struggle with her assailant, the telephone had been knocked to the floor beside her from the small table on which it previously sat. I grabbed it and dialed the Detroit precinct where I used to work, asking for Detective Bill McPherson. Confident he would be on his way, I looked down at Kate again. Her robe was open, exposing the left side of her body. I gingerly lifted the edge of it and covered her bare breast and the area below her waist. The kids shooting marbles flashed in my mind, and I was on my feet in an instant, running toward the stairs and then descending them.

"Hey," I yelled from the door. "Did any of you see someone come out of this building within the last hour?"

All four of them turned to look at me, but said nothing. I repeated the question with urgency. It was the oldest one who then spoke.

"We ain't even been out here for an hour, mister," he said.

"Well, did you see anyone leave since you've been here?" I was yelling, but I couldn't help it. A feeling of wanting to shake the information from him washed over me. "*Just tell me*!" I screamed.

"We ain't seen no one," he said. "What ya gettin' so worked up about? Ya ain't gotta yell like that."

I turned and ran up the steps without saying anything further to the boys. Once back inside Kate Nelson's apartment, I sat on the sofa to wait for the police to arrive, and I allowed myself to do something I hadn't done in years. I buried my face in the palms of my hands and wept.

****

The room was filled with men trying to do their job and I felt as though I were living a nightmare. Mac and his partner, Lawrence Brown, were in Kate's apartment, as well as Wayne County Coroner, Fergus Macgregor. Two uniformed officers stood ready to take orders from the detectives. Two ambulance drivers waited quietly to one side of the room, waiting for Macgregor to give the okay to remove the body of the deceased and transport her to the city morgue. I'd answered all of Mac's questions to the best of my ability. I overheard Fergus tell Mac that the time of death could be anywhere between two to four hours, as he squatted near

Kate, examining the marks on her throat. Looking at my watch, I noted that it was twenty-one minutes after seven.

"Not even as long as that, Doc," I said to him.

The two looked my way and waited for me to explain.

"I talked to her at twenty-five minutes after five this evening. On the phone," I added. "I called her on the phone."

"She say anyone was here with her?" Mac asked.

I shook my head no. Fergus Macgregor rose to a standing position. His eyes remained on the lifeless body of Kate Nelson.

"Nasty business here," he said, scratching his head.

I'd known the medical examiner for ten years now, ever since I'd joined the police force back in 1933. He was a good man. He'd come over from his native Scotland with his parents and ten siblings in 1889, when he was only nine years of age. Now, at sixty-three, his hair was pure white, worn in a crew cut, and his belly had expanded with time. After fifty-four years of living in the States, he'd lost almost his entire Scottish brogue.

Suddenly feeling as though I couldn't breathe, I made my way out into the hall. There I saw Jason Rogers standing in the open doorway of his apartment. He was wearing white socks on his feet and a plaid robe, the sash to it tied around his thick waist. Larry Brown was speaking to him.

I didn't like Larry Brown; I never had. He was Mac's partner now, taking my place when I'd left the department. The guy was a smart aleck; a know it all. I couldn't think of one guy at the precinct who warmed to the man…except the chief. For some reason, the chief liked the guy and had promoted him to homicide detective the same time he promoted Mac. Besides being aggravating, the guy was downright goofy looking, with a head full of brown curls and a wide space between his upper two front teeth.

Reaching in the front pocket on my shirt, I pulled out my cigarettes and lit one with my pack of matches.

"We'll call you if we need you," I heard Brown saying. "Just get back inside."

"Yeah, but what's going on? Is Miss Nelson all right?"

Mac's partner put a hand on the shoulder of Jason Rogers and started to gently shove the man back inside his apartment.

"Brown," I called out. "Just a minute. I'd like to have a word with Mr. Rogers."

The detective looked my way and shook his head as if I were an idiot. He turned and started to walk back to Kate's, but as he passed me, he muttered, "Let it alone, Flanagan. We're handling it now."

I reached the man in the robe across the hall and asked, "Did he even ask you if you saw or heard anything?"

"Saw or heard what? I've been inside here since I got home from work. That was at four thirty. What am I supposed to have seen or heard? What happened over there?" he asked, nodding to apartment 33C.

Before I could answer him, a female voice traveled out into the hall from somewhere inside.

"Sugar plum, come on back to bed. Mama Bear is ready and waiting."

The man's face reddened and he looked over his right shoulder and yelled, "Geez, Janet! I'm talkin' to a guy here at the door!"

"Well, get rid of him, Daddy, 'cause your little girl is hungry."

His face went a deeper shade of crimson and he yelled even louder, "*Will you shaddup*?" He turned back to face me. "Now what in the hell has happened?"

"Somebody got into Kate Nelson's apartment."

"A thief? Did he get away with anything? Did he hurt her?"

"I don't know if he made off with anything, but he did more than hurt her. She's dead, Rogers. Whoever it was strangled her."

In contrast to his coloring just moments before, the man paled.

"Oh, dear God!" he whispered. "Is there anything I can do?"

"You can tell me if you saw or heard anything at all. Have you seen anyone else hanging around here or visiting Kate?"

He was shaking his head.

"Well, listen," I said, removing one of my cards from inside the cellophane of my Lucky Strikes. "Here's where you can reach me. It's got my office number and my home phone on it. Call me if you can think of anything, all right? Anything at all."

He reached out for my business card while his eyes were still trained on the apartment across from his. "Yeah, sure," he muttered.

I turned away from the Rogers residence just in time to see Oliver Treadwell appearing on the third floor of the building. He was the photographer who occupied the office next to mine down on Woodward. He had his camera equipment with him.

"Ollie," I said, surprised to see him here. "You a police photographer now, too?"

"I am when they need me, Mr. Flanagan. What are you doing here?" he asked in his sing-song, slightly feminine voice.

"She was a friend."

"Oh, I'm so sorry."

I followed him in and went directly up to Mac.

"I'm getting out of here," I said. "Call me tomorrow if you need me."

He nodded and I made my way down to the Chevy, lighting another cigarette when I climbed behind the wheel. The boys who'd been playing with their marbles were gone, but there was a crowd of maybe ten people starting to gather outside Kate's building as the sun was sinking in the west. The police vehicles and the coroner's ambulance had peaked their interest.

I didn't start the engine right away, but just sat there with the windows rolled down, smoking and thinking. The more I thought, the angrier I became. There was only one person to whom I'd mentioned Kate Nelson. I'd said I hadn't talked to her yet, but would be meeting with her. I'd alerted him to my plans and, therefore, placed her in danger. The more I thought about the bastard, the more a raging fury rose within me. I was going to pay him an impromptu visit right now. Starting the Chevy, I pulled out into traffic and headed for the Tudor style home on Adelaide.

CHAPTER TWENTY-FOUR

The '38 Chevy came to a screeching halt in front of the Mario Nardini residence. I ran up to that heavy, wrought-iron gate that protected him from the outside world, and rattled it with all my might. There they were, his two flunkies, sitting on the steps of the front porch, wearing their shoulder holsters and smoking their cigarettes.

"Let me in!" I yelled into the yard.

The evening breeze had cooled a bit and the sun had just about bid a farewell to the day. As I stood there, demanding entrance, Mickey and Rico stared at me wearing smirks. Mickey rose and slowly walked toward me.

"What is it now?" he asked. "I don't think you have an appointment, do you?"

"I said let me in! I want to see Nardini right now!"

"Let him in."

The voice came from inside the front yard and to the right. My vision was obscured and I couldn't see who it was, but I knew just the same. It was Mario Nardini.

"Okay, boss," Mickey said over his left shoulder.

He unlatched the gate and I moved past him with speed. The former Purple Gang member was sitting on a black, wrought-iron bench, leaning on a cane which he held in front of him. He was wearing the same gray pajamas and the same dark blue robe. Stopping four feet in front of him, I felt adrenaline surge through me.

"*You're a bastard*!" I screamed.

He nodded his head slowly. "Some have said so."

"First you have one of your goons make a call to me, warning me off this case. When that doesn't work, you have him pay me a visit. Why did you have to kill her? *Why did you have to kill her? I oughta rip your heart out, old man!*"

I took a step toward him and *that* was my mistake. His two gorillas sprang into action; Rico pinning my arms behind me, while Mickey stood in front of me. The bigger of the two cocked a fist and drove it into my gut with brutal force. It all happened so quickly, I didn't have time to react by tightening my abdomen. Two more blows arrived after the first.

"*Enough*!" Nardini called out.

I was released, dropping to my knees as Mickey stepped away. Trying to fight the nausea that was brewing deep inside, I had difficulty inhaling while doubled over. I swallowed hard, willing whatever was rising within me to stay down. It didn't work. Everything I'd ingested in the last twenty-four hours spewed from my mouth, landing just two feet from the old man.

"Pick him up," he said with disgust in his voice. "And clean up this mess."

"Aw, but boss…." Mickey objected.

"Well, then get someone out here to clean it up! Now go!"

Rico and Mickey lifted me by my armpits and set me on the bench next to their employer, and then they crossed the lawn to enter the house. I sank down, still doubled over, trying to recover from the attack.

"Now what's this all about, Mr. Flanagan? Kill her? Kill *who*?"

"You know exactly who," I said weakly. "Kate Nelson."

"Kate Nelson? When and how?"

"Maybe three hours ago. One of your morons strangled her; as if you didn't know."

"Why would I want her dead?"

"Because you're the only one I mentioned her name in front of. I told you I was planning on talking with her. Tonight she told me she thought she knew who Andolucci would take the rap for. Before I got there to hear her story, one of your guys shut her up forever. I'll get you for this, Nardini. You can count on it!"

"Don't be an ass," he said quietly, calmly.

"Who is the kid?" I asked. I wanted to know who Kate had been talking about.

"Billy Levinthal," he said, looking straight ahead, still leaning on his cane.

"Why? *Was* he a kid? Or is that a name he used to be called?"

"Both," Nardini responded. "I don't even think he was twenty years old when he joined the Purples. But we called him The Kid because he looked like he was all of fourteen and no more. And then we joked because of the name Billy. Billy the Kid." He turned to look at me. "Feeling better?"

"Hardly," I said.

"Then go home, Mr. Flanagan. Get a good night's sleep and you'll see how foolish you've been in the morning."

He painfully rose from his position on the bench with the assistance of his cane. Sidestepping the vomit in front of him, he slowly made his way toward the entrance to his house, leaning heavily to the left as he walked.

As I watched him while still seated, I called out, "Remember what I said. I'm coming after you if I find out you're involved."

"And I would expect no less," he called back to me.

****

Parking the auto in the garage, I entered the house from the back door and flipped on the kitchen light. Shamus was lapping up water from his bowl. I made sure the front and back entryways were locked and secured, not wanting to be surprised again by an unwanted visitor; namely Rico or Mickey or both. After getting out of and hanging up my blue suit, I walked to the bathroom in nothing but my boxers and undershirt. I brushed my teeth for a full two minutes, wanting to rid myself of the taste of vomit and Mario Nardini in my mouth. Then I did what any self-respecting private eye would do when he couldn't quite get all the pieces of the puzzle to fit. I went into the pantry and brought my fifth of scotch down from the shelf. Reaching into the cupboard by the sink, I grabbed a tall glass and filled it half full when seated at the kitchen table. I was going to get drunk. It was only nine thirty and I had plenty of time to make a night of it.

Nine thirty—we'd be dancing right now, I figured, Kate and I. She'd wanted to get dressed to the hilt in her fine jade gown. She'd wanted to go out on the town with company she enjoyed. She'd wanted to dance the night away, but she would never dance again. Gone were her desires, hopes, and dreams. Leading someone right to her, I'd allowed him to steal them away. I hated the someone who had killed her, and I'd make sure he paid for it when I figured out who he was.

I wasn't sure what time I blacked out, but I remembered saying aloud to the image of Kate's face in my mind, "Don't die, don't die, don't die." over and over again through tears. It was the second time I'd cried that night.

CHAPTER TWENTY-FIVE

I woke with my head lying on the kitchen table at 8:00 a.m., a kink in my neck making it difficult to rise. It was raining again, the spray entering through the window and causing the curtains, and the floor below them, to get wet. Rectifying the situation, I stiffly moved to shut the window and then headed for the bathroom.

The tightness in my muscles was relaxing under the spray of the hot shower. I spent an extra long time under its flow this morning, not wanting to face the day. When I did emerge, I retrieved my black robe from my closet and covered my body with it. I was hungry and I wanted some coffee, but I didn't want to make it. Instead, I picked up the wet newspaper from the porch and threw it on the end table, and then I lay down on the sofa, resting my head against its arm, and listened to the rain as it pelted the roof. The day was as gray as it could get, robbing me of any inspiration to do anything or go anywhere. I hated what had occurred last night–I hated reliving it in my mind. The only way I knew to escape any vision of the bruised face and neck of Kate Nelson was to allow myself to drift back into a deep slumber.

****

The shrill ringing of the telephone jarred me from sleep with an uncomfortable fluttering in my chest. Not knowing how long it had been ringing, I jumped to my feet and ran to it in the kitchen. It had entered my mind that it might be Mac calling with further questions or additional information for me. I scooped the receiver from its base and breathlessly greeted whoever was on the other end.

"Hello?"

"Hey, you'd better get down here. Something isn't right."

"Who is this?" I asked, feeling as though it didn't sound like Mac.

"Jason Rogers," the man said. "Remember you told me to call you? Well, I just got back from the store and Kate Nelson's door is open a few inches. It wasn't like that when I left. That don't seem right to me."

I blinked the cobwebs away, focusing on what the man was telling me.

"Did you call the police?" I asked.

"Nah, what for…to be insulted by that guy like last night? I thought I'd call you first. I didn't like him."

"You're not alone; no one does. I'll be right there. And listen, Rogers, don't even go near that apartment until I get there."

"You don't have to worry about that," I heard him say right before I hung up.

It was two o'clock when I entered the Somerset Apartments. When I reached the third floor, I saw Jason Rogers standing just outside his doorway. He looked nervous.

"I been standing out here just watching," he said quietly as I neared him. "I don't think anyone is still in there. I haven't heard any noise from over there and I haven't seen anyone come out."

The door to Kate Nelson's apartment stood open about three inches. The cops wouldn't leave it like that, I was sure, and Rogers himself told me it was shut when he'd left the building earlier.

"What time did you leave to go to the store?" I asked him.

"About twelve-fifteen," he said. "I got back about one thirty and called you right away."

"You see anybody hanging around outside when you left or when you came back? Anybody pass you in the hall either time?"

He shook his head. "Nobody passed me in the hall, but Mrs. Sheppard from the first floor was taking out her trash when I went out. You can't tell me she had anything to do with this; she's gotta be ninety years old."

"How about outside?"

"If anyone was hanging around looking suspicious, I didn't notice," he whispered.

"Well, let's go in and take a look," I said.

"Me?"

Rogers was astounded that I would want him to enter the apartment with me. I didn't say anything, but just looked at him. It wasn't working, so I had to plead my case.

"Hey, there's safety in numbers, right? Besides, you said you didn't think anyone was still in there."

"Yeah, but that doesn't mean I'm right. And I think I'd feel a lot safer out here," he said.

"Okay, be that way. But stick around out here so if anybody pops me, you can give the cops a good description of him when he runs out," I said.

His toad-like face took on a look of fear, and I smiled. I braced myself and went in. Rounding the corner and entering Kate's living room, I noticed the small table where her telephone had been overturned. The phone, once again, was lying on the floor. Someone had been there, all right, and it wasn't the cops. Mac's men wouldn't have knocked over the small piece of furniture and just left it like that. My eyes traveled just to the table's left, to where Kate's body was laying the night before, and her face flashed before me for an instant.

"I'm so sorry, Kate," I said in a whisper.

No one was in the apartment—I was almost sure of it—but just to be safe I moved through her bedroom and entered the small bathroom. Both rooms were vacant of an intruder. No one was hiding in the small shower, the closet, nor stretched out under her bed. The woman's evening gown was still lying across it, and I reached down to touch the cool, silky material. She would have looked gorgeous in it. And that's when I noticed the small book lying beside the dress and next to one of the pillows. It was a red leather bound book with the word Diary scrawled across the top in gold lettering. I picked it up and tried to force it into my trouser pocket, but it was too large for the opening. Feeling a bit guilty for wanting to read her words, I pushed that aside, thinking maybe she'd written something about the Kid. Rogers was outside in the hall and I didn't want him to see me leaving with her diary. As if on cue, I heard his voice call out to me.

"Psst...hey, Flanagan!" he said in a loud whisper. "You all right?"

"Yeah," I answered. "I'm coming out."

I found him standing in Kate's doorway. He looked down at the book I was holding. I was carrying it in my left hand, my fingers hiding the word Diary.

"You taking something out of here?" he asked.

"Just a book I loaned her," I lied.

He nodded and backed up to allow me to move into the hallway. I positioned her door to how we had found it.

"Here's what I want you to do, Rogers...."

I didn't have a chance to tell him what I wanted him to do because the door to his own apartment opened.

"Pooh Bear, what's taking so long? I'm in here waiting for you."

My jaw dropped. Standing in the doorway was a beautiful dame, one hot mama with platinum blonde hair and a body that wouldn't quit. She had to be somewhere in her thirties, dressed in some type of red baby-doll lingerie. It was short, showing almost all of her perfectly shaped thighs.

Jason turned to face his wife. He turned the color of a beet. "For God's sake, Janet, get some damn clothes on!"

"What for? And who's your friend?" she asked, leaning against the door jamb with her arms folded across her chest.

He was across the hall in seconds, pushing her inside the apartment. He closed the door and came back to me.

"Hey," he said to me. "You married?" I shook my head and he continued. "Smart boy. Don't do it. But if you ever find yourself wanting to get in that position, don't marry a broad twenty years your junior. It'll kill ya. Now what'd ya want me to do?"

It took me a few seconds to recover from seeing Janet Rogers in *almost* all her splendor. "I want you to go inside, and before you get caught up in anything else, call the police. Ask for Detective Bill McPherson and tell him about the door being open. But don't say you called me first, got it? Don't say I was here."

He was nodding. "I can do that," he said.

****

My watch told me it was twenty minutes to three. I thought I'd swing by the office, but not until I'd had something to eat. I knew just where I wanted to go, and just what I wanted to eat. The Boxcar Café had the best hot ham and cheese sandwiches in the city of Detroit. It was located on Michigan Avenue, just a few doors down from Michigan Central Depot, the train station. It was owned by an elderly man, Charles LePage, and his wife, Ruth. They both had to be in their early seventies, having owned the eatery for the past twenty-five years or more. The restaurant owner went by the name of Spud LePage, because rarely could one find him without a potato and pen knife in his hands. He loved the taste of the vegetable, removing thin slices with the knife and eating them raw.

The café was usually over-crowded at lunch time, but I was entering between lunch and supper, so I had no trouble finding a place to sit. I slid into a corner booth and waited for someone to take my order. Longing for the taste of coffee, I thought better of it, and decided to coat my still slightly upset stomach with a tall glass of milk.

As soon as I told the waitress what I wanted she moved away, and I set the red book on the table in front of me and opened it. Kate Nelson had lovely penmanship, her words being recorded in blue ink. The first page of the diary was dated June 11, 1941. I thumbed through the pages and noted that she wrote in this book every few days. Not wanting to invade her privacy, I went straight to the last few entries. I had first laid eyes on Kate Nelson on Wednesday, July 7. It was hard to believe that only three days had passed since then. I searched for an entry with the same date and found one. It simply read:

Wed. July 7, 1943—If he thinks he's going to send someone here to deliver his messages, he's got a surprise coming!!!!!!!!!! He'd better not be thinking of reneging on paying the rent!!!!!!!!!!

The handwriting on this one was a bit imperfect, the words falling out of the lines. That was the day she'd been drinking in the afternoon. All the exclamation marks told of her anger toward Abe Saperstein. I turned the page and found she'd written in the diary the following night.

Thurs. July 8, 1943—He turned out to be a really nice guy! Not bad looking, either. Well, Kate, it felt good having someone to talk to for a change, now didn't it? Why is it that you feel you have to be a hermit? Maybe it's time to renew your life and start again!

When I turned the page to see if there was another entry, I got a jolt. The page had been hastily torn in two, the bottom half missing.

Fri. July 9, 1943—Well, I did it! I called and I asked him if he wanted to go out tonight and he said YES! So why was I so nervous? It's funny, isn't it? You never know until you try. Besides, I've been thinking and it occurred to me that I might know who Carlo would've been shielding all these years. He talked about him a lot of times when he visited me, so it's got to be th

It's got to be the who? *The Kid*? *Billy Levinthal*? *Who, Kate*? *Damn it*! Someone had gotten into her apartment and ripped the bottom half of this page out. It had to be someone who knew her and knew she kept a diary. Or, did he go to the apartment for something else, and just happened to come across it lying in her bedroom as I had? Kate had the answer for me, but with her death, I wouldn't get to discover that answer, and there were so many more questions.

CHAPTER TWENTY-SIX

After eating, I was feeling much better than I had felt in the last twenty-four hours. I parked the Chevy behind the office building in the lot. Coming around the corner, I spied Hooch Beasle scrambling to retrieve newspapers and magazines that were lying on the ground next to his stand.

"What happened here?" I asked him, noting there wasn't enough wind to cause the periodicals to travel off into the air.

"Eh, some damn idiot came running past here and knocked right into me, sending me into the newsstand," he said, and then he looked up at me embarrassed, realizing he'd used a curse word. "Oh, sorry, Mr. Flanagan."

Something caught my eye out in the street. It was an apple. Apparently, when the stand was knocked over, Hooch's fruit went flying, too. I made a move to go and get it, but a car whizzed past, smashing it under its right front tire before I could reach it.

"Aw, hell!" he said with his hands on his hips, not caring whether he swore or not this time. "I think I lost some coins down into the sewer, too. A whole day's work for nothin'," he complained.

I bent down, picking up the three remaining magazines that were lying out on the sidewalk. One had landed in a puddle which had been formed by that morning's rain. They were issues of The Saturday Evening Post.

"I'll take this one," I said. Reaching into my pocket, I handed the boy a quarter.

"You don't want that one, Mr. Flanagan. It's all wet, and I'm not sure I have the fifteen cents to give you now for change."

"This one will be just fine, and keep the change," I told him. I felt sorry for the boy who was faithfully stationed on this corner to help his mother in supporting the younger children at home.

I climbed the steps to my second story office while fanning the magazine out in front of me, trying to speed the drying process. A faint moaning reached my ears and the noise grew louder as I got closer to the top of the stairs. When I rounded the corner, I saw that Oliver Treadwell's door was fully opened and the sound of distress was coming from within. Stopping when I reached the opened doorway, I peered inside. The chair to his desk was lying on its side and papers were strewn across the floor, along with the camera I'd seen him carry into Kate Nelson's apartment last night.

"What happened in here?"

He turned to face me. "Oh, Mr. Flanagan; someone's been in here! Just look at what they've done!" he whined.

"Anything missing or damaged?" I asked him.

"I don't know. I just got here myself." He bent over and lifted his camera from the floor, turning it over in his stubby hands to inspect it. "I'm not sure, but it seems to be all right," he said. Then he opened the backside of the equipment and peered inside. His face went a shade paler. "Oh no, it's gone! The film is gone! That's why I came in here today, to develop the film from last night."

"Gone?" I asked.

"Yes! What will I tell the detectives? How will they ever trust me again?"

Hooch Beasle's face flashed before my eyes and I took off running for the stairs. I heard Ollie call out to me, but I didn't stop to answer him. The boy was almost finished with packing up his stand for the day when I reached him. I took him by the shoulders, lowering my face to look directly into his own.

"Hooch, listen to me. That guy that you said bumped into you; well, did he come out of my building?"

"I don't know if he came out of your building," he said, startled. "My back was to him, but he came from that same way."

"Did you get a good look at him?"

The boy shook his head. "Not really, why?"

"Now think," I said sternly. "Didn't you look at him at all?"

"Well, yeah, I looked up and yelled at him, but I didn't see his face or anything. He was runnin' real fast."

"Now think!" I said again. "You must have noticed something about him. How tall was he? Was he as tall as me? Did he have dark hair, or light? Can you tell me anything at all about him?"

"Uh, I don't think he was as tall as you, Mr. Flanagan, but he wasn't a short guy, either. And he had on a—"

He was interrupted by his ten-year-old sister, who had just pulled up next to us on her bicycle. She came to a stop and blurted out, "Ma wants you home, Wallace. We're eatin' supper early on account of she has a meetin' at the church tonight. You gotta babysit us."

"Can't you see I'm talkin' to the man? I'll be there when I get there," he said with disgust.

The girl looked nothing like Hooch. Her long braids were light brown and her eyes were a pretty shade of green.

"Ma said *now*!"

He sighed heavily, turning to his sister. "Nora Reese Beasle, if you don't leave me alone, I'm gonna tan your hide when your mama leaves to do her business."

She hopped up on the seat of her bicycle and started to ride off, calling over her shoulder, "Aw, it's *you* whose behind is gonna get tanned! You just wait until I tell her."

Hooch turned back to me, shaking his head. I waited for him to finish his sentence. When he didn't, I had to remind him of what he'd been saying.

"Oh yeah, I was just gonna tell you that he was wearing a dark blue baseball cap. That's all I saw."

Nothing further could be learned from the young man. By the time I reached the photographer's office again, he had it pretty much cleaned up, but he was still in an agitated state over his missing undeveloped film.

"What am I going to do, Mr. Flanagan?" he wailed.

"Ollie, someone wanted that film because maybe he left something behind and he's afraid you captured whatever it was in your pictures. In fact, I'm almost sure of it. Think back and tell me what you took photos of."

His eyes grew wide. "You mean it was the murderer who did this?"

I nodded. In my mind, it all made perfect sense. Coupled with the break-in at Kate's apartment, this guy was running scared because he'd lost something in the struggle with her; something that could link him to her death. Because of what Hooch had told me, I could rule out one person only—Mario Nardini. The man could barely walk let alone run at a fast pace. But he certainly could've sent one, or both, of his bodyguards to do his dirty work. Yet, Hooch had only mentioned one man…so which one was it? I was all for pinning it on Mickey, the big guy. Those punches he'd delivered to me last night, and probably on the previous night in my own home, proved to me he had no trouble inflicting chaos into someone's life. In fact, I wanted it to be him so I could personally bring him down at the end of all of this.

"I took the photos of your friend's body, of course," Ollie replied.

"Did you notice anything else, though? Something lying next to her? Did you take photos of other parts of the apartment?"

My questions put additional stress on the little guy and he became more distraught.

"I don't know, I don't know! I can't *think* right now!" he moaned.

I moved toward him, putting my hand on his back as he buried his face in the palms of his hands while sitting at his desk.

"It's okay, Ollie. Maybe it will come to you. Just let me know if you remember anything."

Making my way farther down the hall, I unlocked my door and threw my hat on top of my filing cabinet. I was angry. Who was doing all of this? I thought I had a good idea, so I decided to put in a call while my blood was still boiling.

The phone was picked up on the fourth ring by the old man himself.

"You're a busy man, Nardini," I said.

"Who is this? Flanagan?"

"Bingo, old man. Now you took something from another friend of mine, and I won't forget this, either."

"What are you talking about this time?" he asked calmly.

"The film. Or maybe you don't know about that one. Maybe your boys realized they'd left something behind at Kate's after they killed her. When they couldn't find it on their return visit to her apartment, they decided to give the crime photographer's office a work over and get the film of the pictures he took last night from his camera."

There was a brief silence. And then Nardini spoke again, very softly.

"You're crazy, Flanagan."

I placed the receiver onto the base of the telephone, ending our connection.

****

Supper was two pieces of toast slathered with peanut butter and grape jelly, and a peach. It was going on nine o'clock and the rain returned. It was more like a mist hanging in the steamy atmosphere. The front windows were open in the parlor and I could hear the whistle of a far off train making its way through the outskirts of Detroit. I sat on the sofa, looking at the two pages of notes I'd written down on my pad of paper. If Nardini and company weren't responsible for all the break-ins and tragedy, then I couldn't think who was. It all pointed to him, unless Billy Levinthal had something to do with this. That's why I'd gone into the office earlier that evening—to see if Frankie had come up with any information on his whereabouts. I figured it was a long shot that she would still be there, but it was worth the try. She wasn't. She'd gone for the day. Tomorrow was Sunday and I wouldn't be any further ahead with information. I'd have to be patient until Monday morning.

I couldn't get it out of my head that the only time I'd mentioned Kate's name was when I was with Nardini at his home. *That's* why he fit. *But why*? What would be his motive? That's what I couldn't come up with. It didn't make sense that he would want Kate dead, that he would be afraid of what she might reveal. I honestly didn't believe Mario Nardini had walked into that restaurant and killed off the man responsible for double-crossing Saperstein, along with Haim Ehrenfeld, and a handful of others on that April evening in 1924. And if I didn't believe that, how could I believe he was behind the things that were happening now?

I was getting a headache. Shutting the notebook and tossing it onto the coffee table, I rubbed at the back of my neck. Maybe if I pushed all thoughts of the case out of my mind for the rest of the night, I could see it from a new angle tomorrow. I'd take a shower, brew a cup of tea, and take it into my bedroom. There, I could read the new Ngaio Marsh novel I had sitting on my nightstand until I fell asleep.

Chapter Twenty-Seven

At thirty-eight minutes after ten o'clock on Sunday morning, I was easing down into a back pew at the First Baptist Church of Detroit located on Woodward Avenue. This was the church that my grandmother and her friend, Helen Foster, attended. I was eight minutes late for the service, and I'd noticed the two women sitting in the third pew from the front when I entered. There was Gran, sitting at the end of the bench, Helen to her right. She always chose the aisle seat, stating that this would make it more convenient if she ever had to visit the ladies room at a moments notice. For some reason, I didn't want them to be aware of my presence.

I hadn't really missed anything, since the congregation was standing with their hands holding hymnals. They were singing "Just As I Am" along with the choir. Benjamin Farron had been the pastor for the past twenty-three years. He was now in his early sixties, married, a father four times over, and the grandfather of fifteen. The man was a nice enough soul and delivered interesting sermons, but I hadn't attended in eight months and, after today, probably wouldn't attend for another eight months. I wasn't trying to avoid him or the Lord; I just felt I had a different type of relationship with my

Maker. But today was different. I felt I needed to sit in God's house to have Him fully hear me.

We sang one more song, me mouthing the lyrics with no sound escaping my lips. Then Pastor Farron moved to the lectern and cleared his throat.

"All of us experience discouragement every so often. Even the most gifted and strong men of God experienced discouragement from time to time," he began. "One of the greatest leaders and motivators of all time taught us how to battle discouragement. Let us learn from his experience. Please turn to Nehemiah, chapter four for this week's lesson."

The sound of people shuffling through the pages of the Bible filled the chapel. The woman sitting to my right noticed I had no holy book and offered to share hers with me, but I declined. She furrowed her eyebrows and then focused on the page facing her.

Pastor Farron continued. "A Christian wife of an unbeliever, a drunkard, and an unfaithful husband, yields to discouragement and the result is a broken marriage, suffering children, and a broken heart. A new believer in Christ gets frustrated and discouraged at his failure to give up old habits and vices, and the result is a lack of growth in his walk with the Lord. A student fails to overcome discouragement because he finds his schooling is difficult, so the result is lack of employment and poverty. But dear brothers and sisters in Christ, we need not yield to discouragement. We are victors in Christ! Let us read from the heart of Nehemiah."

He began to read chapter four, verse one, while the woman sitting next to me, once again, shoved her Bible toward me. I shook my head for a second time and she frowned. Closing my eyes for five seconds, I briefly said my silent prayer—*I'm trying to avoid discouragement, Lord. You're one who believes in justice. Help me solve this case, because I'm getting nowhere on my own. Amen.* I then slid out of the pew and left the church.

I was back home and in my robe, searching the contents of the icebox, by fifteen minutes after eleven. There wasn't much there and I really didn't feel like fixing anything, but I was starving. So I pulled out the eggs and cheese and made myself two fried egg sandwiches. Placing them on a plate, I carried it along with my novel to the front room. Reclining against the arm of the sofa with my legs spread across to the other end, I ate the sandwiches while I read. Unlike yesterday, there wasn't a cloud in the sky. The temperature and humidity had lowered and I was enjoying this weather. I wasn't going to worry about who had killed my father or Kate Nelson today. For now, I felt I'd already left that in the hands of the Lord.

****

When the call came in, I'd been immersed in an episode of The Shadow. A bit annoyed that someone would be phoning in the middle of the program, I made my way to the instrument on the back kitchen wall.

"Hello?" I said, letting my irritation show.

"Mr. Flanagan?"

"Yeah?"

"This is Oliver Treadwell. I hope I'm not disturbing you. You sound a little perturbed."

"Oh, Ollie; no, you're not disturbing me."

"Well, I hate to give you bad news, but I've wracked my brain trying to think if there could have been something belonging to the killer on that roll of film and I can't come up with anything."

"Well, you gave it your best shot, Ollie. Don't worry about it."

"Like I said, I just photographed the victim. She did have a pearl earring lying by her body, and her necklace was near the wall I think, but that was it. I'm so sorry."

"That must've happened in the struggle," I replied. "If anything further occurs to you, just let me know."

He agreed and we rang off. I was back at the wireless in plenty of time to hear the conclusion to "Isle of Fear."

CHAPTER TWENTY-EIGHT

Monday morning's weather was a replay of the previous day. Maybe the heat wave we'd been experiencing since mid-June had ended for the time being. One could only hope. Looking out the kitchen window, I could see the trees in the backyard of the Randle residence fluttering with the strong winds. I drank the last of the coffee in my cup and reached for the keys to the Chevy, anxious to get to the office. It was going on ten o'clock...I'd slept late.

****

As I reached the second floor and rounded the corner, heading toward my door, I stopped dead in my tracks. Coming out of Ollie's office was Mickey, the man employed as Mario Nardini's bodyguard. What in the hell was he doing there? He was heading for the stairs, but before he passed me, he looked straight into my eyes, tipped his fedora, and smiled. When I recovered, I rushed to the photographer's door and barged in. I'm not sure what I'd expected...another mess covering the floor, or worse yet, the lifeless body of Oliver Treadwell? Instead, I found Ollie sitting behind his desk, holding a check in his squat fingers. He looked up when I entered.

"Mr. Flanagan," he said in a hoarse whisper. "Some man was just here and gave me this. He said his boss heard about my troubles and wanted to help out with any cleaning or repairs I might have to make. Look."

I edged closer to where he sat and he turned it around for me to see. It was a check signed by Mario Nardini for one hundred dollars. I let go of a soft whistle. How about that? This guy was foxy. Either he was as guilty as hell, or he was stupid with generosity. I couldn't figure out which.

A couple of bills were shoved under my door. I bent to pick them up, throwing them onto my desk, and then removed my hat and placed it on top of the filing cabinet. I was thinking of strolling across the hall to see Frankie when she appeared in my doorway with a sheet of paper in her hand.

"Well, I found something out on your man, but I'm not sure it will help you," she said.

She sat down in the chair facing me at the desk and began to tell me what she had learned.

"First," she said, "William Isadore Levinthal was born in Milwaukee, Wisconsin on February 12, 1905. It seems he left Detroit to go back home in the spring of 1934 and got a job in his father's printing business. There, he met a woman and married her a year later, only it wasn't a happy union. He got nasty when he drank, which was all too often. The last time he beat her up, he broke her jaw. It was the straw that broke the camel's back, so she left him, which was in 1939. Seems his father wasn't too happy with him, either. He didn't like the way his son was running his personal life, and didn't like his lack of productivity on the job, so he fired him. After failing at one job after another, he voluntarily signed up with the army in late December of '41. Last known, his unit was stationed in Belgium."

Well, hell, there went another possibility of who could be behind the recent happenings. When was I going to get a break?

"How'd you find all this out?" I asked Frankie.

"I called his older brother Moses in Milwaukee," she said.

"You think he's on the level?"

"I had no reason to doubt him," she responded.

I rubbed my chin, deep in thought, as she rose and went to the door, stopping as she reached it. She turned around to say something.

"Oh, and you owe me for the long distance call."

"How about I repay you by taking you out to lunch?" I suggested.

She pondered that for a moment and began to nod her head in assent.

"That might work," she said.

"Today?"

"Nope."

And then she was gone, heading back to the office of Irwin Malcolm Wright. Without an idea of where to go next with this investigation, I put in a call to Mac at the station. He told me of the break-in at Kate's apartment, but said he couldn't figure what the guy was after. Except for the overturned table, the place looked the same as when they'd left it. When I asked him if they had bagged anything besides the woman's body, he told me his partner, Larry Brown, had been in charge of that.

"I think there was only some of her jewelry lying close by," he said. "I believe it was a pearl earring or something like that. Listen, Sam, I know she was a friend and it's hard. I just want you to know however long it takes, we'll get him. We're working on it."

With lack of direction, I decided to straighten my files, which took me all of fifteen minutes. At ten minutes to noon, the phone rang.

"Is this the detective?" an elderly woman's voice asked when I had answered the instrument.

"Yes, ma'am. This is Sam Flanagan."

"Well, I need to hire you. My eggs are missing."

"Your what?" I asked, thinking I'd heard her wrong.

"My eggs are missing and I know who did it. He keeps coming in here in the middle of the night and he takes things. Yesterday I couldn't find my crochet hook. I live alone and it frightens me. I've called other detectives, but it seems no one is willing to help."

I held the receiver away from my ear and frowned at it. *Eggs? Crochet hook?*

"Okay, so who do you think is doing it?"

"Mr. Tanninger. He lives next door with that floozy wife of his."

I asked for her name and address and jotted it down on a notepad. No ideas were coming to me on the case I was presently working on, so I might as well take on that puzzle. I was hoping I could clear this up with one visit to the man in question. Promising to look into it, I told her I would probably swing by her place later that afternoon. After disconnecting, I hauled the telephone directory out of the bottom drawer of the filing cabinet and turned to the T's. There was a Lloyd Tanninger listed on the street she had given me. I wrote his address down. The only thing was I didn't feel like making the trip out there. Maybe I could solve it just by talking to the man over the phone. I dialed the number.

"Hello?" a female voice said.

"Uh, hello ma'am, I'm looking for a Lloyd Tanninger. Is he there?"

I heard a soft gasp travel through the line.

"Lloyd?" she asked.

"Yes, ma'am."

"Who is this?"

She sounded upset suddenly, almost as though she was on the verge of tears. Cautiously, I proceeded.

"Uh, ma'am, if I could just speak to him for a moment."

"Is this some type of sick joke? My Lloyd is gone. He died three weeks ago. Now who *is* this?"

Stunned, I made my apologies and told her I must have the wrong Lloyd Tanninger and hung up. Taking the paper with the old woman's address on it, I balled it up and threw it in the waste paper basket. She was missing a lot more than her eggs!

For the next two hours I sat in my office behind my desk and thought back to all those I'd spoken with since I'd started this investigation. A strong sense that I was missing something filled me…there were things that people had told me that weren't jiving. And as hard as I tried, I couldn't put my finger on what those things were.

CHAPTER TWENTY-NINE

My grandmother called the house at almost half past four.

"Sam?" she whispered. "Come get me, and when you get here, say I'm needed at home."

"Why?" I asked.

"Tell you later, dear," she said, and then she hung up.

"You want to tell me what that was all about?" I asked Gran as she sat next to me in the Chevy. We were pulling out of Helen's driveway.

"She gets on my nerves," she said. "She won't let me do a thing! She makes breakfast, cleans up afterwards, and does it all again at lunch and suppertime. She tells me I'm her guest and she just wants me to sit in that lousy chair and relax all day long."

I looked at her, stunned. "Before you were complaining that she made you do everything."

"Oh, I was not," she replied, and I rolled my eyes.

We ate supper at five thirty and then spent the early evening in the parlor reading—well, I was reading. Gran was looking at the pictures in the magazine I'd purchased from Hooch. She couldn't see well enough to read the articles. I was captivated by my Ngaio Marsh novel when my grandmother said something to me. Looking over the top of the book, I asked her to repeat what she'd just said.

"I asked you who this man is. The way he's standing there, it looks like he thinks he's the cat's meow."

Rising from the chair, I crossed the room to her. Looking at the page that was opened, I saw the Italian leader gazing back at me, arms folded across his chest, his chin in the air.

"Oh, that's Mussolini," I told her.

"Well, who is he?"

"Gran," I said, surprised she didn't know. "That's the guy running Italy."

"Oh," she said with distaste. "Well, he looks like a real numbskull."

"He is."

Returning to my chair, I once again picked up my book. I began to read where I'd left off, but now I couldn't concentrate. Something was bothering me. I went to my bedroom to get my pad where I'd jotted my notes. Reading over my conversation with Herschel Sussermann, what entered my mind wasn't recorded there. Something Sussermann had said at The Double Shot that night I'd been there surfaced in my mind, and I could hear him saying it, plain as day. "We could hear him yelling through two walls, and when I looked up, the kid was all wide-eyed and had an uncomfortable look on his face. I remember Abe telling where the mark would be the next night, and I believe he said he'd be at La Bella Luna."

A jolt ran through my body as I realized for the first time that someone else was with Sussermann when Saperstein was ranting in the inner office! Another Purple Gang member knew *who* was to get hit, *when* he was to get hit, and *where* the hit would take place! And the older bookkeeper had referred to him as the "kid," the same as Kate had done. But it wasn't the Kid, as in Billy Levinthal, because he was inside that inner office at the time. Was there another member who was quite young? Who was it?

Adrenaline surged through my veins. I was hopped up with excitement. I returned to the room where Gran was sitting, still thumbing through the pages of The Saturday Evening Post.

"Gran, I have to run out for a bit. Do you think you'll be all right if I leave you alone?"

She looked at me over the top of the magazine. "Well, of course I will. It'll be good to have some time to myself."

"When I leave, I want you to lock the door after me," I told her.

I grabbed my hat and keys and was out the back heading for the garage a moment later.

****

The Double Shot was rather crowded for a Monday evening. Two women and a man sat next to each other at the bar. None of them appeared too happy. Two couples occupied one of the square tables in front of the window. They seemed a bit more jovial. Three men, probably in their sixties, stood at the end of the bar nursing frosted glass mugs of beer. They were debating with each other over something and I heard one of them loudly say, "Eh, you're full of shit!" Looking toward the booth that Sussermann had been in when I'd last spoken with him, I found it to be empty. My watch read twenty-three minutes after seven. The bar owner had told me the old gent came in five nights a week at precisely seven thirty and left at eight fifteen.

Neamon waved as I entered and I made my way to the stool I'd occupied the last time I was there, the one by the cash register.

"Give me a scotch on the rocks," I told him.

"Will do," he said, and turned to lift a glass from the shelf above him.

I sat, sipping on my scotch, and frequently turned toward the door.

"Expecting someone, Sam?" Neamon asked.

"I need to speak to Sussermann."

He nodded and meandered down the bar with a towel in his hand. The two women rose from their table and headed for the jukebox. They inserted a coin and I heard the upbeat tune of "College Rhythm," sung by The Three Cheers, fill the room. Inside, my heart was fluttering with anticipation. I glanced at my watch again...only four minutes had passed. Pulling out a Lucky Strike, I lit it and inhaled deeply.

The men down at the end of the counter were getting louder and I looked their way.

"You're damn right I would! If I were a younger man, I'd have my rear end over there and kill every one of them damn Nazis, and then I'd head to wherever those Japs are and mow them down, too!"

"Oh sure! You'd do it all singlehandedly! Just drink your beer and keep your mouth shut!"

Neamon noticed my gaze and came to stand in front of me, leaning on the counter. "Eh, don't worry about them. They come in here twice a week and have the same argument each time. After their five beers, they'll leave while singin' songs with their arms around each other."

I looked toward the entrance again. It was seven thirty-seven. Sussermann was late and I was beginning to worry. I looked at Neamon and he shrugged, a concerned look on his own face. Trying to calm myself, I sipped at my drink and smoked my cigarette. Paul Tremaine started singing "Stormy Weather" and the two women began to dance with each other at their table. Neamon was still leaning in front of me.

"Uh, what happened?" he asked, gesturing to my face.

My hand traveled up to my left cheekbone. "Oh this? Some guy got a good punch in. You should've seen it before the swelling went down."

"Your job is dangerous."

I nodded. "Yeah, it can be."

The sound of the door opening reached my ears and I turned, seeing Herschel Sussermann pass through its opening. I hadn't realized I'd been so tense and holding my breath, but I let it out now with a sigh of relief. Neamon smiled and called out to him.

"Hey, you're late. I'll have your drink over to you in a minute."

The old man nodded and slid into his seat after depositing his cane and hat in the booth behind him. I strolled over, my own drink in hand and carrying my cigarette. Herschel Sussermann had the same fraying gray suit on. He wore the white shirt and red bow tie. The man also wore the same dark glasses as I'd seen him wear last time.

"Excuse me; Mr. Sussermann? I'm not sure if you remember me, but I spoke with you a week ago here. May I have a word with you again?"

He motioned with his hand for me to have a seat, and I slid in across from him.

"Are you the man who knows my Eliana?" he asked.

"Well, I didn't really *know* her," I said, and left it at that. "What I wanted to speak to you about was how Abe Saperstein ordered that hit at La Bella Luna years ago. Do you remember us talking about that?"

"Ah, yes," he said. "I remember you now. You were asking about that young man who worked for Abe. That one who was a foreigner."

"Yes," I said, feeling elated that this man remembered. "You told me that when Abe was screaming in the office, the kid was all wide-eyed and uncomfortable looking. Someone was sitting out there with you. Who was that? Was that another Purple Gang member who was with you that day?"

"Ah, yes," he said. "He'd come in with the young foreign fellow that day. He was sitting across from me while I sat at my desk. That was—"

"Here's your drink, Mr. Sussermann," Neamon said, placing the martini glass in front of the older man.

"Do I owe you anything for that?"

"Nope, it's all taken care of. The olives are in the bottom of the glass. I still don't have any toothpicks. I hope that's all right."

"That's just fine, Mr. Riley," Sussermann answered.

Neamon turned and moved away from the table. Now I could find out who overheard Saperstein rant in his office that day. Now I could find out the name of someone else who knew about the hit, and where and when it was to be.

"You were saying, sir?" I prompted him.

"Saying?"

"You were about to tell me who was in the outer office with you that day when Abe Saperstein was ordering the hit at La Bella Luna. You referred to him as 'kid' before."

The man suddenly took on a look of sadness. "Eliana wanted children quite badly. I didn't mean for it to turn out the way it did, but there was nothing to be done about it. It was my fault you know. The doctor said so. No, no, young man; we couldn't have kids. And it was all my fault."

He moved his fingers, searching for his glass. When they touched the stem, he cautiously lifted it to his mouth and took a sip.

"No, sir, I was asking who the kid was who was sitting across from you in your outer office the day that Abe Saperstein was yelling about someone stealing from him. Who was that? What was his name? He was another member of the Purple Gang. Who was he?"

"I didn't like Abe. He was Eliana's brother though, and I didn't want to cause trouble. He was mean, real mean. They should all rot in hell. Each and every one of the Saperstein boys."

"But who was the *kid*?" My voice had risen. I was sorry as soon as I had asked the question in that tone of voice, but I couldn't help it. I needed this information!

Under his dark glasses, the man's left eye began to twitch, and not just slightly.

"I told you, young man; we couldn't have kids."

If it hadn't been for the fact that I would be hauled off to the penitentiary for the rest of my life, I would've gotten out of the booth, taken Neamon Riley by the front of his shirt, and beaten him to within an inch of his life.

CHAPTER THIRTY

I woke Tuesday, July the thirteenth, feeling like crap. Physically, I was all right, except for the headache that was slowly traveling up from the back of my neck. More to the point, I was still upset about last night and my lack of success with Herschel Sussermann. When I climbed out of bed at a few minutes after eight, I immediately went to the kitchen and drank Bromo-Seltzer for my breakfast.

The day was gorgeous. Soft, billowy, clouds rolled by in the light blue sky and the temperature was in the low seventies. It didn't erase my mood, though. I was in a funk and I wasn't going to climb out of it any time soon. Maybe I didn't want to. I'd been working on this case for more than a week straight. The money that Sophia Andolucci had paid me was used up, and so was my patience. I felt as though I didn't want to go on spinning in circles on this one, and I wasn't going to. Mac would be working on the murder of Kate Nelson and I would leave it to him. If and when he solved that, maybe it would clear up who had killed my father. The thought of going into the office today didn't even enter my mind.

Gran carried her cup of coffee and a small bowl containing two hard-boiled eggs into the parlor where I sat.

"I boiled some eggs, dear," she said. "Don't you want any coffee?"

"I'll get some in a minute."

"Are you going into the office?" she asked.

"Nope."

"Oh good, then maybe you can take me to the market, dear. I need to get some groceries."

Oh that's just great, I thought; but I didn't say it out loud.

****

We were home by two thirty. Gran was in the kitchen unpacking the bags and I was $16.81 poorer. I'd stayed out in the Chevy with the windows down, smoking, while she did her shopping. As soon as we'd gotten back home, I headed straight for my bedroom to lie down on top of the made bed. My hands linked behind my head, I stared at the ceiling. Who was it that was sitting across from the bookkeeper on that day back in 1924? Herschel Sussermann sure couldn't tell me. Certain memories which were deep in the old man's mind would stay locked away forever. The only one I knew to ask was Mario Nardini. Hopefully, he would know. But contacting him after I'd gotten angry with him didn't seem to be an option. Not yet, anyway. Maybe if I put some time and distance between us I could do that at some point, but not right now. I didn't want to admit it, but so far I had failed at this one. Rising from my position, I went to the phone and dialed Sophia's apartment. It rang nine times and then I replaced the receiver. I'd try again later. Sitting around feeling frustrated and sorry for myself wasn't my style, so I decided to work in the yard. It had been a whole week since the lawn had been given any attention.

At four thirty I reentered the house, the grass looking good again. I dialed Sophia's once more. This time she answered.

"I'd like to stop by if I could," I told her after we greeted one another.

"Any time is fine," she said. "I just got home from work and have no other plans for tonight. Do you have new information for me, Mr. Flanagan?"

"We can discuss it when I get there," I told her.

When I disconnected, I became aware of voices coming from the front room. Gran was having a conversation with someone. I went to see who it was and saw Augie sitting in the chair by the end table. I said hello to the big guy and he nodded.

"Augie's been visiting," Gran said. "But he went out just now and his tire is flat. He doesn't have a spare. Can you give him a ride to the restaurant?"

I spied his auto parked at the curb across the street through the front window.

"I can do that," I said.

"Good! I'll come with you and we can have dinner there."

"We just bought all those groceries," I said.

"They'll keep," Gran reasoned as she headed for the bathroom. "I'm in the mood for another pizza."

My grandmother slid into the back seat, freeing up the front so Augie could sit there. He surprised me by climbing in next to her. She was taken by surprise, too.

"Oh good, what fun! Sam can be our chauffeur and we can pretend he's taking us some place!"

I looked in the rearview mirror at her. "I *am* taking you some place," I said.

"Oh, I know; but you know what I mean."

These two were foiling my plans. I really needed to swing by Sophia's to talk to her and I didn't think it would take long, so I asked if they would mind a stop along the way. They said they didn't mind; or rather Gran did. I guess she looked to Augie for his consent, and he must have agreed with a nod of his head.

I parked on the street right in front of the Harrington Arms Apartments and turned the engine off. Gran was peering out the window at the building.

"She lives here?" she asked.

"Yeah," I said.

The back door of the Chevy opened and I looked behind me.

"What are you doing?" I asked when I saw my grandmother exit the vehicle.

"I've never been in an apartment," she said.

"Well, you're not going in one now, either. Gran, this is business. I can't take you in there with me."

"Oh, all right," she said with disappointment. "Come on, Augie. We'll just walk through the halls then."

Without a word, the man got out of the car. I rolled my eyes. Geez, this guy was turning out to be her lapdog.

Nito answered my knock and ushered me into the apartment. Did the man live here? The first time I came to see Sophia, I was under the impression he lived elsewhere. Maybe I'd been mistaken. He either lived with his sister, or couldn't seem to keep away from her. As I entered the living room, I heard the woman's voice coming from the kitchen.

"I don't understand you, Nito. How could you have broken it? You haven't taken that off since Mama and Papa gave it to you over twenty-five years ago."

"Hey," he called out. "Can we drop it? Flanagan is here."

She came into the room wiping her hands on the light green apron she was wearing. She greeted me, saying she hadn't expected me so soon, and I'd caught her in the middle of preparing dinner. After she invited me to have a seat, I told her the reason for my visit...that I was giving up the case.

Working for a week on it, I'd made headway. I was convinced that Carlo Andolucci hadn't committed the murders at La Bella Luna, but that was the extent of any success in my investigation. There was nowhere else to turn in finding out who the real shooter was. A brick wall stood between me and any further information. She was extremely disappointed.

"No, I'll pay you more money," she said. "I want you to continue."

"Sis, listen; the guy said he's hit a brick wall. You can't keep giving him your hard earned dough when he can't solve it," Nito said.

I turned to him, not liking the sound of what he'd just said, but he was right. So far, this case seemed way out of my reach. The sun streaming in hit his ring, the one with the small diamond in it, and shone in my face for an instant.

Turning to face the woman again, I said, "He's right. I'm not getting anywhere with this. Maybe I can pick it up again at some point."

She stood. "No," she said adamantly. "I'm paying you for a few more days. Just stick with it, and if you don't find anything further, you can take a break then for the time being."

She left the room and Nito sighed, shaking his head. He picked up a magazine, the same Saturday Evening Post Gran had been holding in her hands last night, and began to thumb through the pages. Would *he* know who Mussolini was, I wondered?

I noticed the ring again; I'd seen it the first time I'd been there, along with the silver chain he wore around his neck. He wasn't wearing the chain today. An itch started to crawl up my spine. And then suddenly, it was as if I was viewing a newsreel being played right before my eyes.

Sophia returned to stand at my side, handing me four ten dollar bills. As if in a trance, I took them from her, placing the money in my top shirt pocket. She took her seat and started to talk, but I wasn't hearing her. My gaze rested on her brother once more.

The image of my grandmother last night flashed before me. She wanted to know who Mussolini was—Benito Mussolini. Things were occurring to me at a rapid pace. Kate's words sounded in my ears…*I think his name was Buddy, or maybe Benny or Billy; something like that.* She said it all made sense to her who Carlo would protect, and it was all suddenly making sense to me, too. From what I had learned of Carlo "the Confessor" Andolucci, he was very family oriented. Only family would motivate him. He would only protect family. I thought back to the last time I was there and how Kate had called me at that location. My God, I'd mentioned her name, along with what time I'd pick her up…all with Nito—Benito—a room away! He hadn't been asleep on the couch. He only wanted me to think he'd drifted off. He'd heard every word said. Mac only mentioned an earring that was bagged. That idiot Lawrence Brown missed getting the necklace lying up against the wall. It wasn't Kate's necklace; she had no other jewelry besides that one pair of earrings. She'd told me that herself. Nito's chain was lying in that apartment, and he'd gone back to retrieve it. He'd found it and it was now probably lying in a drawer at his place, broken. He had to next get that film out of Ollie's camera. He couldn't have the police seeing they'd missed a piece of evidence…evidence that wasn't in the apartment anymore. And that's what Sophia had been complaining about when I walked in moments ago…his broken chain. And that's why he was eager to shut her up in front of me.

I looked at the ring on the third finger of his right hand yet again. It would sure be a good substitute for a pair of brass knuckles.

My God, it was Nito who had gone into La Bella Luna that evening. He would've been what, sixteen at the time? Just a kid in the eyes of many. Understanding of why Carlo Andolucci had taken Nito's place in jail filled me. After all, he'd been a second father to the young man. I was sure he'd loved his wife's brother, and mentioned him frequently while visiting Kate Nelson in her apartment. And I was sure he felt it would destroy the woman he loved if she found her brother had committed such a heinous act. What I *didn't* understand was why this man who sat across from me felt he had to take it upon himself to carry out the hit ordered by the leader of the Purple Gang, Abe Saperstein.

Turning to Sophia, I interrupted her flow of words. "You really should have left this alone," I told her.

The frail Sicilian woman looked confused, and I saw out of the corner of my eye that Nito had lifted his head to stare at me.

"Why? Why would you say that, Mr. Flanagan?"

"Because I know who murdered those people in the restaurant, and it wasn't your husband," I said quietly.

"You do?" she asked, surprised.

I focused my attention on the man who'd just tossed the magazine he'd been holding onto the coffee table.

"Did Carlo ever call you Benny?"

He said nothing, but fear flickered briefly in his eyes. Sophia laughed.

"How did you know that, Mr. Flanagan?" she asked, smiling. "Carlo's the only one who ever called him that."

"Shut up, Sis!"

"Nito, what's the matter with you?" she asked in a wounded voice.

"I'll tell you what the matter with him is. He allowed your husband to go to prison for an act which he, himself, committed. He also killed Kate Nelson a few days ago and he knows I'm aware of it."

She gasped. "Nito, is this true?"

Sophia Andolucci and I stared at the man while he stared back at me. His face was showing signs of anger and his breathing was accelerating. He appeared to be a desperate animal that was caught in a trap, with nowhere to escape to and nowhere to hide. I actually jumped when he threw his head back and growled loudly. It was a sound I'd never heard emitted from a human being before. I tensed, ready for him to attack, but he didn't. He brought his head forward, buried his face in the palms of his hands, and began to cry.

"Why'd you do it?" I asked him quietly.

Through his sobs, he answered. "Because I knew he wouldn't! And if he wouldn't do it, they'd kill him! I loved him!"

Sadness coursed through my veins. Sophia's brother had tried to protect the man he had come to know as his second father. He hadn't realized that the order for this hit wasn't being given to Carlo Andolucci, but to Billy Levinthal instead. Carlo, in turn, somehow found out about Nito's involvement and had protected his wife and her brother by taking the blame and going to prison for a crime he hadn't committed, and years later, losing his life there. Kate Nelson had been pulled into this whole mess by me and had paid for it with her own life. My parents, along with a handful of others, had been at the wrong place at the wrong time. And now Sophia would be without the brother she loved. Everyone was a loser in this one.

"Call the police," I said quietly to Sophia.

Without a word she left the room, void of emotion, looking more drained and frail than I'd ever seen her. I kept my eyes trained on Nito, who had lifted his face from behind his hands and just stared straight ahead, tears inching down his cheeks.

Sophia was returning to the living room...I could hear her footsteps. She hadn't been gone long enough to make a call. Suddenly, I caught sight of an object being thrown past the left side of my head and landing at the feet of Nito. The coffee table obscured my view of what it was.

"Hurry, Nito!" she yelled.

The man reached for what was on the floor and got to his feet in an instant. He was half-way across the room before I figured out he was holding a butcher knife in his right hand. The only thing I had time to do was to raise both feet and shove them into his stomach as he approached me. He went flying backward and fell onto the table. I jumped up, preparing for another attack from him. As he lumbered to his feet, holding the knife high above his head, his sister jumped on my back.

"I won't lose you, too, Nito!" she screamed. "Kill him!"

She then leaned in and bit my left ear as I struggled to shake her loose. It was that struggling on my part that prevented the blade from entering any deeper than it did. I felt a searing heat run through my left shoulder while the woman lost her grip on me and slid down to the floor. Now free of her, I cocked a fist and pushed it into the left side of Nito's head, but it wasn't a direct hit and it only knocked him off balance. So I did the only other thing I could think of. Brother and sister were both caught off guard by me shouting at the top of my lungs.

"AUGIE! AUGIE!"

The big guy burst through the door to Sophia Andolucci's apartment. He lifted her brother off the ground from under his armpits and threw him onto the couch, then bent down, picking up the butcher knife that had fallen from Nito's hand. My grandmother arrived on the scene just as Augie straightened from grabbing the weapon. She watched as Sophia tried to lift herself off the floor.

"Oh, here dear, let me help you. How in the world did you end up down there?" Ruby Flanagan then looked at me and sighed with disgust. "Oh, Sam! Just look at the new shirt I just bought you. You've got it all ripped and stained with blood!"

CHAPTER THIRTY-ONE

"Sam? Sam, are you ever going to wake up? It's past noon and I haven't heard a peep out of you," my grandmother said while bending over me at my bedside.

I struggled to open my eyes, turning to my nightstand clock after doing so. The clock told me it was eleven minutes past twelve. Yawning, I blinked a few times before I felt as though the stupor was clearing in my head.

"I guess those pain pills the doctor gave me do more than ease the pain," I told my grandmother.

"Well, try to sit up, dear. I'm going to fix you some breakfast and bring it in here on a tray."

Before she could leave, I called to her. "Hey, Gran? I love you, you know."

She blushed. "Well, I love you too, dear," she said.

I laughed. "And I think I'm beginning to love Augustino Consiglio. He's my hero."

Breakfast was oatmeal pancakes with maple syrup, crisp bacon, tomato juice, and coffee, and I ate it all in the comfort of my own bedroom. Birds were singing from the elm tree that stood about eight feet from my window on the front lawn. The sun was shining brightly from a cloudless sky, and I could tell from the lack of a breeze and the climbing humidity that the higher temperatures were returning. Gran brought me the morning paper and I read it, turning the pages with my right hand as it lay across my lap. My left arm was in a sling. Despite my injury, my mood was light and cheery. The killer of my father and Kate Nelson was behind bars, and hopefully, so was his sister, Sophia Andolucci.

Augie had phoned the police station from Sophia's apartment. He kept his eyes on Nito the whole time he was speaking into the instrument, and the murderer knew better than to make a move.

I'd arrived home from the hospital emergency room last night by taxi at a quarter of nine. Gran had been waiting for me, arriving about twenty minutes earlier. Augie had driven me to the medical facility, and then drove my car to his place of business. I urged him to take my grandmother along with him, allowing her to eat her pizza. There was nothing she could do by staying with me. I gave her one of the ten dollar bills Sophia had given me–no way I'd returned it to her–telling Gran to get whatever she wanted. At closing time, Augie drove her home, with his brother, Dominic Consiglio, following so he could take Augie home. My car was now safely tucked away in the garage.

Every time I thought of how I had wanted to tell my grandmother and her friend to stay in the auto when we'd reached the Harrington Arms Apartments yesterday…well, I now shuddered at the thought. There were times when one had to accept that Divine Guidance played a role in decision-making, and this was one of those times. After folding up the Detroit News, I took the time to thank the Lord for His intervention.

I made my way to the bathroom to relieve myself and to wash up. With only one hand available, it was more difficult than I thought it would be. The burning and achiness in my shoulder seemed to be rearing its ugly head again, so I took two more pain tablets before I returned to my room. It wasn't long before the grogginess kicked in and I drifted back into a deep sleep.

****

When I woke, it was going on five o'clock. At first, I thought my grandmother was entertaining company; but when I left my bedroom to visit the bathroom once again, I saw that she was on the telephone.

"Oh wait, he's up now. Let me ask him." She put her palm over the mouth-piece. "This is Helen asking if I'm going to the evening service tonight. I told her I should probably stay here with you. What do you think, dear?"

Forgetting my shoulder, I shrugged, and then winced with the pain. "Go if you want, Gran. I'll be fine."

It was settled; Gran was going to attend church that evening and I would take advantage of the peace and quiet to finish the novel I'd been reading. I was looking forward to it. But first, I wanted to check in with Mac at the station to find out what was happening. I dialed the precinct while my grandmother was locked behind the bathroom door and in the tub.

"Hey Mac, how do they like the inside of a cell?" I asked him after he came on the line.

"Hey there, Sam; uh….," he started off nervously. "I hate to tell you this, but we had to release them."

"*What?*"

"Their story is that you flipped your lid, accusing Nito of killing your father and the Nelson woman. Then you grabbed a knife from the kitchen, threatening the man with it. He tried to grab it from you and somehow you ended up getting cut in the struggle."

"They're lying!" I said loudly.

"They're both saying it, and they haven't wavered one bit in their story."

"Hey, whose side are you on? I didn't touch that knife. Check the prints on the handle."

"We did. There are plenty of prints on the handle, including the huge palm print of your friend there. They're all smudged now because of him holding the knife in that palm. Yours could've been among them."

My blood was boiling. "You're making me mad, Mac! I didn't touch that knife and I'm not lying to you."

"Now settle down, Sam. I know you better than that. I'm just giving you the facts. I believe you. But she called in some high-falutin defense attorney, and he told them both to clam up for now, and he bailed them out. We have nothing concrete to hold them on...not *yet*, anyway. Have patience; we'll get them."

When Mac told me the attorney's name, I was floored. The guy was well known in Detroit for getting scum off without even a slap on the wrist. In fact, I couldn't think of a case he'd ever lost. I hung up after Mac told me to keep the faith; there was a first time for everything. But, in this instance, I had no faith to keep.

I didn't tell Gran about this latest development; I let her leave with Helen thinking everything was hunky-dory. After she was gone, I sat in the parlor, holding Shamus in my lap and looked out the front window, stewing over what Mac had told me. My ex-partner was a good detective, but the lawyer he'd named was even better at what he did for a living. I knew that and I knew what I had to do. Reasoning with myself, I tried to talk myself out of it. It wasn't working. Emotion was leading me right now. Placing the cat on the floor, I made my way to the kitchen and dialed the number of Mario Nardini. He picked up after the first ring.

"This is Flanagan," I said. "Remember you wanted to know when I found out who Andolucci was protecting?"

"Yes," he said quietly.

"Well, I don't know the guy's last name but it's Nito, Sophia's brother. He killed my father and he killed Kate Nelson." And then I suddenly got nervous and wasn't sure I was doing the right thing. "But tell me Nardini...what are you going to do? I mean...well, I need to know. Are you really going to just talk to him?"

I waited for an answer, but none came. He'd hung up after he'd received the information he'd been waiting for. In a panic, I redialed his home. No one answered.

****

Gran returned home just before eight thirty. While she was gone, I'd spent an emotional roller coaster of a night. I was antsy.

"Hey, remember when you told me you'd give anything to take a ride in the back of your father's buggy one more time?"

She replaced her teacup in its saucer and smiled, nodding her head.

"Well, let's do it," I suggested.

"But where would we get the horses, dear?"

"Not horses, Gran. I've got the Chevy. You can get dressed in your nightgown and sit in the back seat. Bring a pillow and I'll put the window down so the air hits you in the face. Let's take off tonight about midnight and head on down to Grover Hill."

Grover Hill was a small village in Ohio at a distance of just under a hundred and fifty miles from Detroit, heading southwest. My mother lived with her only daughter there. Eva's husband, Clifford Deans, was the only dentist in town.

"To see your mother and Eva?" she said. "We can't, dear. Who would take care of Shamus?"

"I can run next door and give the key to Albie. He'll watch him. That kid is always looking for a way to make some coins," I suggested.

"What about church on Sunday?"

"Oh, don't worry about church on Sunday. Besides, we'll probably be back before then. Let's go and stay two or three nights. It's only Wednesday. And, Gran, Ma and Eva deserve to hear what really happened at La Bella Luna."

Ruby Flanagan's face brightened and she brought her hands together in a clap, but just as suddenly, she frowned.

"But your arm, dear. You can't drive like that. And those pills make you sleepy."

"I can drive with one hand, and I won't take the pills. I'll be fine until we get to Eva's," I said.

"Let's do it!" she said. She was on her feet heading for her bedroom. "I've got to pack!"

Forty-five minutes later, my grandmother's small suitcase was lying on the couch, with a very old and dusty rag doll sitting on top of it. I asked her about it, where she'd gotten it.

"Papa got us each one for the Christmas of 1871. I'll never forget it. It was the best Christmas I've ever had. I named her Poppy because she used to have hair the color of the poppies in the field surrounding our house back then. I've had her in the back of my closet for years, but I think she wants to go with us tonight."

There was the gleam of excitement on Gran's face. *Everyone should live their lives through the eyes of a child with no worries; no tough decisions to make*, I thought…just as Ruby Flanagan did.

EPILOGUE

We were back in Detroit and in the comfort of our own home late Saturday evening. Gran was pleased that she wouldn't miss the Sunday morning service with her friend, Helen Foster.

The trip to see my mother and Eva had been the right decision to make. I'd felt more relaxed than I had in a very long time. Cliff and I got in some fishing time at a small lake nearby; well, at least *he* did. My shoulder and arm still weren't up to par, so I sat next to him as he caught Friday evening's dinner. My mother and grandmother shed tears and clung to one another right before we pulled away from the house on E. Perry Street, and I vowed to not let months lapse before another trip was made to see them.

The call from Mac came in late Sunday morning. My grandmother had left with Helen to head to the First Baptist Church of Detroit on Woodward Avenue, and I was enjoying a second cup of coffee while finally finishing the book I'd started days ago. I recognized his voice right away.

"Hi." My tone was reserved.

"I've been trying to get hold of you."

"Gran and I went down to Eva's," I said, not elaborating.

"Well, that accounts for you not being at the Nelson showing or funeral. I wondered where you were. You should've seen it; flowers galore, showy casket, the works. She was laid out Thursday and buried at Woodmere Friday morning."

"Her ex-husband arrange it?" I asked.

"Not unless she used to be married to Mario Nardini," he said.

Nardini? Now that one stunned me.

"Well, if that's all, Mac—"

"Now, hold on," he interrupted me. "I know you're still upset with me, so let me just emphasize that I believe you when you say the guy is guilty of the shooting and he's the one who killed your friend. We just have to *prove it*, that's all. You remember how that goes, don't you?"

"Yeah."

"Well, there's more evidence against him."

The beats of my heart picked up speed. I was curious as to what other evidence there was that pointed toward Nito's guilt.

"What?" I asked with eagerness. The chill I'd felt toward my ex-partner was beginning to melt.

"He's run off," he said.

"What do you mean, 'run off'?" I was beginning to get a strange sensation making its way up my spine.

"Yeah, he took off. No one can find him, and he must've been in a real hurry, because he didn't take a thing with him. His sister is worried...says she hasn't seen him since Wednesday evening. Her brother said he was going to have a few drinks at a neighborhood bar and that's the last she's seen of him. The bar owner says he never came in. I guess he didn't trust the hot-shot attorney."

"Hmm, guess not," I muttered.

"I just wanted to let you know what's been happening. And, Sam, this isn't over yet. We'll get him, my friend. Count on it."

I received another call just before nine o'clock on the evening of Tuesday, the 20th of July. Neamon Riley called to inform me of the passing of Mr. Herschel Sussermann the day before. I took the news harder than I thought I would. Each of the people whom I had spoken with regarding this case—Herschel Sussermann, Neamon Riley, Mario Nardini, Arthur Nass, Ulysses Wright, and Kate Nelson—had given me vital information. Their tidbits were pieces of a puzzle that, when put together, formed the whole picture. I was indebted to them all. Even Gran played a small role in asking about Benito Mussolini. And Augie…well, he truly was the reason I was breathing now. There was something I was leaving undone and I vowed to correct that the following morning.

****

Wednesday it would be another scorcher. Already eighty-six degrees, it was only ten minutes to nine in the morning. I put my empty coffee cup and saucer in the sink and headed out to the garage. Before I arrived at the office for the day, I wanted to make one stop. I'd found out which plot Kate Nelson was buried in at Woodmere Cemetery; it wasn't hard to do. Pulling up in the Chevy, I noticed the sleek, black limousine with Rico and Mickey leaning against it, cigarettes hanging out of their mouths. We ignored each other as I made my way up the shallow hill. Mario Nardini stood at the base of her grave, leaning on his cane. I was a bit out of sorts, not expecting to find him there. Reaching the grave, I stood beside him. He glanced at me and nodded, and then returned his gaze downward to the blanket of flowers that covered her plot.

"So you did this for her?" I asked, not knowing if he would answer.

"Someone had to." He sighed. "I put in a call to Saperstein out in New Jersey. He never offered. In fact, seemed rather relieved he would no longer be paying rent or sending money."

"She was better than that." I said. "Kate was too good for him."

Nardini was nodding his head. "That she was, my friend."

It wasn't lost on me…his calling me "friend." I was a little more than surprised after all I'd accused him of. He pivoted with difficulty and made a move to descend the hill to his automobile. I turned and called after him.

"Nardini, did you have that talk with Nito?"

He stopped and faced me over his shoulder, shaking his head.

"No, I never talked to him."

"Well, did you send those two after him?" I nodded in the direction of his bodyguards. "Please. I've got to know."

He seemed to study my face. Then his lips curled into a slight smile. He tipped his hat and said, "Maybe I'll see you around sometime, Flanagan."

Watching him travel painfully down to his car and the two men whom he employed, I half expected him to lose his balance and roll down the hill. I didn't turn my attention to Kate until the limousine had disappeared from sight. When I did turn around, I noticed the headstone for the very first time. It was solid black marble with her name, Kathleen P. Nelson, etched on it. Below her name was the dates of her birth and death; May 20, 1898-July 9, 1943. A lovely angel was carved into the base of the stone.

In our privacy, I told her I was sorry, and I thanked her for all she'd been to me, however briefly. I thanked her for her help with the puzzle. And I let her know that she would've looked gorgeous in that jade evening gown while standing behind a microphone on a stage.

"What song would you have sung to me, Kate?"

****

By two in the afternoon, I'd had it. Not one single call had come in to Flanagan Investigations, I was sweating like a pig due to the high heat and humidity in my office, and because Frankie was out with the flu, Irwin Malcolm Wright was staring at me while sitting behind her desk from across the hall. I was going home!

I pulled up to the house on St. Aubin and found Augie's car parked at the curb, but it was his brother, Dominic, who sat next to Gran on the sofa in the parlor. He had her hands in his.

"Oh please, beautiful lady; just consider it," he was saying.

"Consider what?" I asked as I tossed my fedora on the dining room table.

He looked up and let go of his hold on her.

"I'm trying to talk your lovely grandmother into taking a position at 'Augie's Cuchina'," he said.

"Taking a position?" Stunned, I moved into the room where they were and took a seat. Moving the ashtray from the end table to the arm of the chair, I pulled out a Lucky Strike and lit it. "What's this all about?"

"Augie needs to get out of that kitchen, because I have to return to my own job. What better than to have his wonderful baking teacher take his place?"

I was astounded. Gran wasn't going to work for Augie; not at her age! Dominic pushed on, naming the amount she would be paid. It was way too low. Shaking my head, I told him so, but I could see excitement on my grandmother's face.

"Gran, you're not really considering this, are you?"

"Well, dear, I could help out with the bills around here."

"Not on *that* amount, you couldn't. Besides, let's face facts. You're eighty-two years old. It would be too strenuous on you. No way are you going to go to work at this time in your life."

Dominic made one more plea. "How about this…you work only two days a week. Pick your own days even. Augie pays you what I said, and you also get to take a couple dozen peanut butter cookies home with you each week. Would that work?"

My eyes widened a bit. I was a sucker for peanut butter cookies. They'd always been my favorite.

"Oh, Sam is right. I *am* gettin' up there in age, and then there's always the fact I've never held a job in all my life."

They both turned to stare at me when I said, "Now wait, Gran. I mean, if it's only two days a week…you could at least *try* it, couldn't you? Maybe we're being a little hasty."

ABOUT THE AUTHOR

Judith G. White holds a degree in secondary education with a major in history from Western Michigan University. She currently works part time at The Henry Ford, America's Greatest History Attraction, where her life has been enriched by meeting dignitaries, entertainment personalities and leaders in business and industry. She's traveled throughout the lower forty eight states and toured Great Britain. History, reading, playing word and trivia games and, of course, writing, is what she likes to do best. She makes her home in a southern suburb of Detroit along with her husband, Jim; two children, Brandon and Erin; and two dogs, Sadie and Orie.

Facebook author page:
https://www.facebook.com/SamFlanaganmysteries

Other Sam Flanagan mysteries:
A Method to Madness: The Case Files of Sam Flanagan
Sins of the Father: The Case Files of Sam Flanagan

www.ingramcontent.com/pod-product-compliance
Lightning Source LLC
Chambersburg PA
CBHW050027180626
46810CB00002B/606